To Emma,

Missing Beat

Bob Stone

'Listen to your heart'

Beaten Track
www.beatentrackpublishing.com

Missing Beat

First published 2018 by Beaten Track Publishing
Copyright © 2018 Bob Stone

ISBN: 978 1 78645 198 9

Beaten Track Publishing,
Burscough, Lancashire.
www.beatentrackpublishing.com

Dedication

To Wendy, for whom my heart beats.

Acknowledgements

Turning a vague idea into a finished story, and then seeing it become the book you now hold in your hand, has been an incredible process, but one which would have been impossible without the support and encouragement of many incredible friends, who would not listen to my excuses and made me not just finish the book, but do something with it. If I were to list them all here, you would never get to read the story, so the old 'you know who you are' will have to suffice. I trust that you *do* know who you are, because you have my love and gratitude forever.

I do have to single out Debbie McGowan, the brilliant publisher at Beaten Track, for a special mention, though, because without her faith, you would not be reading this now. Debbie is the most supportive, patient and often good-humoured publisher/editor I could have wished for, and I will always bless the day I met her.

I also owe a huge thank you to the immensely talented Trevor Howarth, who took a very vague brief and turned it into the stunning cover which graces this book. He can be contacted at wowhow@icloud.com.

One other person who thoroughly deserves their own mention is my wonderful wife Wendy. Never have the words 'without whom' meant so much. Without her, I would simply do nothing.

Contents

Part One 1

    Chapter One 3

    Chapter Two 7

    Chapter Three 11

    Chapter Four 15

    Chapter Five 19

    Chapter Six 23

    Chapter Seven 29

    Chapter Eight 35

    Chapter Nine 39

    Chapter Ten 43

    Chapter Eleven 47

    Chapter Twelve 51

    Chapter Thirteen 55

    Chapter Fourteen 59

    Chapter Fifteen 63

    Chapter Sixteen 67

    Chapter Seventeen 73

    Chapter Eighteen 81

    Chapter Nineteen 83

    Chapter Twenty 87

    Chapter Twenty-One 91

    Chapter Twenty-Two 95

    Chapter Twenty-Three 99

    Chapter Twenty-Four 103

    Chapter Twenty-Five 107

    Chapter Twenty-Six 111

Part Two **113**

    Chapter One 115

    Chapter Two 119

    Chapter Three 123

    Chapter Four 129

    Chapter Five 133

    Chapter Six 139

    Chapter Seven 143

    Chapter Eight 147

    Chapter Nine 153

    Chapter Ten 157

    Chapter Eleven 161

    Chapter Twelve 165

    Chapter Thirteen 169

    Chapter Fourteen 173

    Chapter Fifteen 179

    Chapter Sixteen 185

    Chapter Seventeen 189

    Chapter Eighteen 193

    Chapter Nineteen 197

    Chapter Twenty 201

    Chapter Twenty-One 205

    Chapter Twenty-Two 209

    Chapter Twenty-Three 213

    Chapter Twenty-Four 217

    Chapter Twenty-Five 219

Epilogue **221**

About the Author **223**

By the Author **224**

Beaten Track Publishing **225**

PART ONE

Chapter One

*L*ISTEN...
Joey Cale was listening to his heart instead of paying attention and did not see the silver BMW hurtling towards him until it was too late.

Listen...

For as long as he could remember, he'd been aware of his heart. It wasn't really his choice, but something which had been drummed into him by his parents from when he was small. "Listen to your heart," they said, especially his mother. "Tell us if you hear anything different." So Joey listened, but all he could hear most of the time was a regular *dub dub*, just like everyone else.

Joey was different, he knew that. When he was six or seven and the other kids were out playing football or rounders in the street, he was never encouraged to join in. On the rare occasions he did go out, his mother watched from the window, so he never stayed out long. He sat inside with his books, listening to the excited shouts of the other kids outside and longing to be out there with them.

You have to watch your heart was a phrase Joey's mother used over and over again. Any time he tried to do anything strenuous, his mother was always there, saying, "You have to watch your heart." The doctor had said Joey was fine now and there was no need. But *watch your heart* became the soundtrack to Joey's early years—the pale, weedy kid who watched the other kids play from the sidelines or inside.

Would he have been allowed a normal life if his granddad had not died so suddenly? Joey couldn't be sure. He'd never really known his mum's dad, only a vague recollection of a short, old man in a cardigan. Granddad Williams had died when Joey was five, just dropped down dead in the street. A heart attack, they said. He would never have known what happened. But Joey knew what happened because his mum never, ever got tired of telling him.

You have to watch your heart...

Look what happened to your granddad.

Joey couldn't really blame his mum. He'd been born prematurely, by caesarean section, and complications with his birth had, he'd been told, meant both he and his mum had nearly died. She'd been in a coma for over a week while Joey spent the first weeks of his life in an incubator. He'd been born with VSD—a hole in his heart—and it had been serious enough for him to need an operation at three months old, an event Joey remembered nothing about.

It had healed well, the doctors said, but even though the check-ups grew less frequent over the years, it didn't stop his mum watching him, especially after Granddad Williams dropped dead. Joey's mum carried her guilt at not being there for the first days of his life like a lead weight, and nothing his dad or anyone else could say could convince her it wasn't her fault.

Now Joey was older, he understood more about the operation. There was, after all, plenty of information on the internet. He knew that, to all intents and purposes, he was cured. But years of reinforcement by his mum had created habits, and Joey still listened to his heart.

Still regular, still just *dub dub* like everyone else's.

And yet...

Sometimes, very rarely, Joey heard something different. Usually, when he was stressed or nervous about something—like that time he found himself alone with Harriet Fforde and had no idea what to say—or if he'd been running, there was a different sound. Sometimes he felt his heart miss a beat.

People sang about it in cheesy old love songs, the kind his dad liked to play in the garage.

But it's a bit different when you feel it yourself.

When you're used to listening to your heart because you've been brought up to worry that one day it might just...

Stop.

That moment when it seems to pause is truly frightening. For the briefest of moments, the thought flashes through your head what if... But then your heart starts again; the rhythm is back, and you forget about it until the next time.

Sometimes Joey went for days, weeks even, without giving his heart the slightest thought. There was too much else to think about—A' Level results, uni, how his mum would cope without being able to fuss over him if he got into Newcastle like he wanted...

Perhaps if he had not had all these distractions, he might not have been listening to his heart the day his A' Level results came out, and he'd have seen the silver BMW.

Perhaps, if he'd been paying attention, Joey Cale might not have ended up among The Missing.

Chapter Two

W HEN JOEY WOKE up that morning, it took several minutes to register that this was the day. Results day. He nearly turned over and went back to sleep, but then his mum called him, and it was all too real.

"Joey! It's eight o'clock. You don't want to be late!"

As if he would. He knew that people would be turning up all morning to get their results, and being among the first would only mean queuing, but his parents insisted he got there for nine. That way, he could meet them for lunch to celebrate and then go and see his friends later. They only ever talked about 'celebrating', as if the alternative didn't exist.

The idea of getting together with loads of friends was a ridiculous one too. He knew some of the other sixth-formers had things planned, but Joey had not been invited to any of those; he rarely was. He would probably meet up with Sam later, and they would go for a burger or something, but the cooler set, who would be meeting up at Chris Barrett's house or going to Wetherspoons to see if they could get served, never included Joey. Truth be told, he wasn't bothered. He would be quite happy if he got his grades and went off to uni and never saw any of them again.

That was what happened if you never joined in. If you never took part in the football games at primary school, by the time you went to senior school, no-one asked you any more. Joey didn't really care. He didn't like football or the other stupid games they played. He spent his breaks in conversation with Sam, his only real friend, talking about books or music or films. It was like they were invisible, which suited them both perfectly. Sam didn't mix much because of his stammer, even though, like Joey's heart, it had got better over the years. People still called him 'S-S-Sam' sometimes, but mostly they just left Joey and Sam alone.

Joey didn't rush getting showered and dressed. He wanted to leave as little time as possible between coming down and leaving the house. His parents would be bags of nerves, and he wanted to stay calm. He thought he'd done well enough in his A' Levels; that was one advantage to never being invited anywhere: you got the work done. There was still a nagging doubt, though. Newcastle wanted two 'B's and a 'C', but what if he had missed by just one grade? There was always Clearing, but he didn't really want to think about that.

He could smell coffee as he came downstairs, and someone had burned the toast. His parents were both in the kitchen, and his mum greeted him with a hug.

"Big day." She clung to him as if her life depended on it.

"Should be okay," Joey replied, his voice muffled by his mum's hair. When she finally let him go, her eyes were damp and glistening.

"Breakfast?" his dad asked. Ian Cale was not really one to show his feelings, unlike Joey's mum. It seemed like Barbara Cale had to show everything the second she felt it.

"I'll just have cereal, thanks." Joey reached for the cornflakes packet and tipped some into his bowl while his dad poured him a cup of tea. Joey wasn't a fan; he'd read somewhere that tea was as much of a stimulant as coffee, but his mum wouldn't believe it and rarely allowed him to have coffee. Whenever Joey met up with Sam, he always drank it. He sometimes wondered if his mum could smell it on his breath when he came back, like she would if he'd been smoking or drinking.

"You should have some toast, too," his mum said. "You need something inside you."

"I'm fine with this, Mum. Honest."

"I know, but—"

"I'm just going to the school to get handed an envelope. Toast won't change what's in it."

"I still remember going for mine," his dad said. "They posted them all up in the woodwork room window. That way, you could get your results without having to bump into any of the teachers. They were all hiding in the staffroom."

"I know, Dad," Joey groaned. "You said." He finished his cereal and looked at his watch. "I'd better get off. I'm meeting Sam in a bit."

"Don't forget your phone," his mum said. "Have you got credit on it?"

"Yes. And I charged it."

"And you will ring us, won't you? As soon as you've got your results?"

"Yes, Mum."

"Because I know what you kids are like. You'll get talking to your mates and forget."

Joey had to smile at that as he picked his phone up and put it in his coat pocket. *If you knew what us kids are like, you'd know I haven't really got any friends to get talking to apart from Sam.* He grabbed his keys and called, "Speak to you in a bit!" as he headed for the door. He didn't want any more hugs. There would definitely be tears this time.

His parents chorused, "Good luck," to him as he hurried out of the house. He sent Sam a quick *on way* text and set off for the school. It was only a ten-minute walk, and he was early, so he took his time, slowing as he passed the newsagent. He thought about stopping to see if his *Doctor Who* magazine was in yet, but Mr. Ashraf was outside, straightening the papers.

"Good morning, Joey. Big day today, isn't it?"

"Yes, it is, Mr. A. Just heading there now."

"Well, good luck. You'll be fine. You work hard, Joey, not like some." He nodded towards the photocopied 'Missing' poster in his window.

The poster was yellowed and faded; Emma Winrush's face had been looking out of that window for months. She'd gone to a different school to Joey, so he didn't really know her. He thought he'd seen her around; her purple hair and goth eyeliner made her stand out, and, of course, her face was everywhere when she disappeared. But she'd never turned up and was old news now.

Joey said goodbye to Mr. A. and carried on to school. He could always pop in for his magazine later. As he rounded the corner and the school came into view, ahead of him, other kids wandered along in groups of two or three, chatting to each other or on their mobiles. It was a 'big day' for all of them, one way or another.

Sam was waiting on the corner, and Joey gave him a half wave. He could feel his heartbeat speeding up the nearer he got to the school and was listening intently to it as he approached the junction before the school gates. The traffic lights were about to change, and Joey sped up so he wouldn't have to wait. He didn't see the silver BMW jump the lights. He only heard the squeal of brakes as the driver slammed on and felt his heart stop dead.

Chapter Three

JOEY THOUGHT HE must have blacked out or something when his heart stopped. He heard the screech of car brakes, could still hear it. He thought he might have heard someone shout. Then he must have passed out. That was the only possible explanation. He had to be dreaming now. That thing his mum had feared for so many years had finally, actually happened, and the shock had made his heart stop.

He was either dead or in a coma. But if he was dead, why could he still hear his heart? It was there, steady as ever, so...maybe he was in a coma. Because what he saw when he opened his eyes could not possibly be real. He was still there, standing in the middle of the road, but everything seemed to have stopped. It just wasn't possible.

Joey closed his eyes again, as if that would change the view next time he opened them. But the view was the same. All the other kids heading for the school were gone. All the passers-by who had been on the road were gone. All the cars jostling for position to get through the lights first were...

"Still there," he whispered. Queued but not moving. At first, he thought the traffic was snarled up as it sometimes was at that junction, but when he looked closer, he saw exactly why the cars weren't moving. They were all empty, as if they'd been abandoned right where they were. There was no engine noise, no honks of horns, no sound at all.

Get out of the road! his brain urged, but then it asked, *Why? The cars aren't moving.* Then it froze altogether, and he stood there, rooted to the spot. No people. Just Joey, on his own, in the middle of one of the busiest roads, surrounded by an eerie silence.

It took a few seconds—which felt far, far longer—for time to unfreeze and Joey to step back onto the pavement. He looked around. The main road stretched a long way in both directions, with no sign of people, or moving vehicles or noise. Automatically, he took his phone out of his pocket to see if there was a message from Sam or anyone which might explain what was going on.

He remembered this one time when the police closed the main road for some reason, and for a while, it had been deserted, like it was now, except it hadn't been a minute ago.

So...what? An accident?

But there were no messages, no missed calls. Battery was fine, but there were no signal bars. *Typical.* Just when he needed it, the network looked like it had dropped out. With no real idea where to go or what to do, Joey did the most obvious and natural thing. He headed for home.

His mind was so distracted by the bizarre lack of human life, it took him a while to notice something else that, when he did finally notice, it was both blindingly obvious and impossible to take in. It was only when he nearly walked past the newsagent without recognising it that the truth dawned on him. The shop which, not fifteen minutes earlier, had been called 'Ashraf's' was now apparently called 'Benson's News' and had a completely different display in the window. There was no yellowing poster of the missing Emma Winrush, nothing which appeared remotely familiar from the view he had seen earlier. On an impulse, Joey pushed the door, half expecting it to be locked. But the door opened easily and Joey went in.

"Mr. A?" he called, but there was no answer. "Hello?" he called again. "Mr. A?"

Joey glanced round at the displays, looking for something tangible for his brain to seize on, and found it on a nearby shelf. *Doctor Who* magazine—the new issue he had thought about buying earlier. Seeking familiarity, he took the magazine from the shelf and studied the cover. What he saw again made him feel as though the ground had shifted under his feet. Filling the cover was a face he had never seen before and the words 'Brian Black Is The Doctor!'

The only possibility Joey could comprehend was that it was a joke or a hoax. The fact that, for the first time ever, a female actor had been cast in the title role of his favourite show had been all over the press. There had been complaints and controversy, but if the BBC had changed their minds, surely Joey would have heard. He turned the pages; there was a long interview with plenty of photographs of this actor Joey had never heard of, who had been cast as the eleventh Doctor—

Eleventh? Thirteenth, surely!

Joey dropped the magazine as if it was hot and fled from the shop. Once outside, he broke into a run and kept his head down. He didn't want to see anything else until he reached the sanctuary of his house.

Chapter Four

WHEN JOEY REACHED his front gate, he checked his phone again. Still no messages and no signal. He took out his key, opened the door and went inside, closing the door firmly behind him.

"Mum? Dad?"

He paused, but there was no answer. *They must have gone out.* Joey went into the kitchen and shook the kettle. *Empty.* He filled it at the sink and switched it on, then sat on a chair at the kitchen table. He was confused, but above all angry that, instead of waiting for him to come back with his results, his parents had chosen to go out to Tesco or somewhere. There again, they always left a note on the kitchen table to say where they'd gone. Joey usually sent a text, but they always left a paper note. Joey checked the table again in case he'd missed something, but there was no note. He hoped there hadn't been a problem with his gran. But if something had happened, his mum would have left a note, even if it only said 'be back later'.

When the kettle clicked off, Joey got up, took his favourite mug out of the cupboard—a TARDIS mug with square sides, which made it harder to drink from but looked really cool—shook some instant coffee granules into it and filled it with water. It was only when he went to put the lid back on the coffee jar that he noticed his mum had changed brand. They always had Nescafé. *Always.* Dad was always complaining that Mum never bought shops' own brand products, always spending more on big names.

"You get what you pay for," she always said.

His dad always replied, "Try telling the bank that."

It was like a running joke. Yet this coffee was called Maxcafé and clearly a rip-off of Nescafé, because the label design and logo were almost exactly the same. Maybe that was what had fooled Mum. Joey sniffed the coffee and took a sip; it tasted pretty much the same too.

He took his coffee through to the living room, where he settled into his favourite armchair and pointed the remote, thinking there might be something on the news to explain the empty streets. If not, there was bound to be an episode of *The Big Bang Theory* on one of the channels, even if it was one he'd seen before. But typical of today, there seemed to be something wrong with the television, and the screen was filled with white static. He could make out a picture in the background, but it looked like a snowstorm.

Joey checked the cables in case his mum had knocked something when she was hoovering—as she sometimes did—but everything seemed to be as it should. His efforts having made no difference, he turned the TV off, tossed the remote on the coffee table and sat back in his chair with his coffee to think and wait.

Fifteen minutes later, he was bored of waiting. He checked his phone again—still nothing—and got up. He stood in the living room, no idea what to do next. Perhaps he should ring someone to see if he could find out where his parents were. Not the police; it was far too soon for that. There was one other obvious choice, and he knew the number by heart; he retraced his steps to the landline phone by the kitchen door.

If his parents were visiting the home where his gran had lived for the past two years, at least he would know they'd be back before too long. He picked up the handset and put it to his ear. But instead of the dial tone, there was a crackling hiss, like the noise the television had made. He listened to it for a few seconds because there was something else there. In the background, behind the hiss, he thought he heard a very faint voice. He couldn't make out any words, but it was definitely someone speaking, like the sound of someone in another room with thick walls between. The hiss grew louder and louder until it drowned out the voice. Joey quickly put the phone down. So much for that idea.

Now he really didn't have a clue what to do. The house was silent and felt odd. There was a chill in the air, despite the weather being warm outside, and it reminded Joey of something, but he wasn't sure what. Then it came to him. The house felt like it did after they had been away on holiday, sort of cold and unlived-in. It always felt like that until a door or window had been opened and someone let warm air in.

Joey went to the back door, turned the key, pulled back the bolts and opened it, stepping outside into the small back garden. The air certainly felt warmer out there, but like everywhere else, it was silent. A busy road ran at the back of the house and there was always traffic noise, even if you stopped noticing it. Now, there was nothing. Joey waited and listened, but there was no noise at all. No traffic, no birdsong, nothing. A cold, hard ball of anxiety began to form in the pit of his stomach. There was something really wrong, and he didn't know what it was, or what to do about it. He stood there, in the garden, with tears prickling the backs of his eyes. He'd never felt so alone in his life.

Chapter Five

TWO HOURS LATER, there was still no sign of Joey's parents. Joey had spent the time wandering through the house in case there were any clues as to their whereabouts, though he had no real idea of what he was looking for. Their suitcases were still where they lived, on top of the wardrobe, so they hadn't just run off, not that this was at all likely. Everything was just as it should be but felt slightly *off* in a way Joey couldn't put his finger on.

No further on, he went back downstairs to wait some more. He tried to read a book, but the words wouldn't go in. It was only when he picked up a newspaper to flick through that he began to understand that something was *really* wrong, and again, just as he had when he looked at the magazine in the newsagent's, he felt his world lurch.

The front-page headline and story of the newspaper was all about the president of the USA visiting Britain. Joey didn't take a great deal of interest in the news, finding it all too depressing, so he hadn't been aware the president was due to visit. But that wasn't what caused the feeling of the ground dropping out from beneath him. It was the picture that accompanied the article. Whoever the man in the picture was, he was definitely not Donald Trump. He was an older, bearded man, whose name seemed to be Irving.

Joey dropped the paper and felt a sudden, uncontrollable urge to get out of the house. This was not right. His world was not right, and he needed to know why. He grabbed his keys and coat and hurried out of the door, slamming it behind him. The slam echoed in the empty street, and Joey looked left and right with no idea where to go next.

He stopped on the pavement and took a deep breath. There was something wrong with the time, as well. It should have been early afternoon by Joey's reckoning, but the sky looked more like late evening. He looked at his watch, but it seemed to have stopped a few hours ago, and he wondered if maybe he'd fallen asleep at some point without realising it.

He stood in indecision, like an idiot, for a minute or so, then gritted his teeth. There had to be something sensible he could do. He looked up and down the street again. There were several cars stopped in the middle of the road, but there were also cars parked outside most of the houses. *Somebody* had to be in.

Joey pushed open the gate to the next house. Jim and Moira had lived there for years, and he knew them well. He knocked on the door, aware, from past experience, that the bell didn't work. He waited. There was no answer, so he knocked again. Still no reply. He moved on to the next house. A couple whose names he did not know had recently moved in with two small children and an obnoxious yappy dog. Joey always said hello when he passed them in the street, and they always returned the greeting, but that was the extent of the conversation.

He pressed the bell button and heard a chime ring somewhere in the house. No answer. Not even the dog. The next house belonged to an elderly lady named Mrs. May who rarely went out unless her family came to take her somewhere. Joey knocked loudly on the door, because Mrs. May was hard of hearing and, because she walked with a stick, he waited a bit longer this time. But just as before, there was no-one in.

Joey was considering whether to try every house in the street or give up, when he caught something out of the corner of his eye. He could have sworn he saw movement in the distance, a fleeting glimpse of what looked like someone hurrying away. It was so quick he couldn't be sure, but in case he was right, he shouted, "Hey!" and sprinted to the end of the road, where he stopped and looked both ways, but there was no-one. The road at the end of Joey's was a cul-de-sac, so there was only one direction the person—if there was a person—could have gone, and that was into Bridge Street, which ran parallel to Joey's.

He rounded the corner and looked down Bridge Street. Whoever it was couldn't have got far, but there was no sign of life. Just in case, Joey shouted, "Hey!" again, but there was no answer. *I must've imagined it*, he thought and would have turned to go back the way he'd come, except something made him stop dead.

There, on the pavement, was a cigarette butt. It was not unusual in itself, but this one had faint tendrils of smoke drifting from it, and the tip still glowed in the inexplicable dusk. Joey crouched down and picked it up. He wasn't seeing things. The cigarette had been discarded within the last minute or so. Someone *had* been there. Joey dropped it back on the pavement and ground it out with his foot.

"I know you're there!" He walked down the street, looking all around, and then paused to listen for any sign of movement. "Where are you? I need to talk to you!"

He walked a bit further, peering in through the windows of the houses he passed, but they all appeared as dead and deserted as his own.

"Come on!" he called again. "I saw your cigarette. I just want to talk!"

There. A noise behind him. He turned and barely had time to register the fact that there were two figures advancing on him, before one of them grabbed his jacket and slammed him into the wall. Joey was hit by a wave of stench, the smell of dirt and body odour and neglect, and a face came up close to his. The man was filthy, dressed in grime-encrusted clothes, and had matted, tangled long hair.

"What you got?" he hissed into Joey's face, his breath rank.

"I-I haven't got anything!" Joey stammered, struggling to break free of the man's hold. Behind his assailant, Joey could see the second man, slightly shorter, but just as much of a shambles.

"What you got?" the man pinning Joey to the wall repeated.

"Nothing! I haven't got anything!"

Joey struggled against the man's grip, and, finding strength he didn't know he had, shoved him backwards. The man stumbled into his friend, and Joey backed away, frantically searching the road for the best way to escape.

The last thing he expected was for someone to grab his arm from behind. It felt like his heart had stopped again, and it was all he could do not to scream as he was dragged roughly into a narrow alley.

"What the hell do you think you're doing?" a voice hissed. "Get in here, dickhead."

Joey jerked his arm to pull himself free. "Get off! What are *you* doing?"

"Saving your life," the voice, now recognisably female replied. "We need to get inside before dark. Are you insane?"

Now he had his arm free and could take a step back, Joey was able to see the person who had grabbed him. She was shorter than him, with untidy purple hair. Even with fury etched on her face and none of the heavy make-up he was used to seeing on posters, it only took Joey a second to realise that he was looking at the missing Emma Winrush.

Chapter Six

THERE WAS NO time to ask questions. He could hear the footsteps of his two attackers following but didn't dare look behind him as Emma—if it *was* Emma—dragged him down the alleyway and in through the back door of a house. She slammed the door shut and bolted it at the top and bottom. Joey squinted into the gloom while Emma hurried around the room—a kitchen, he thought—pulling down blinds. He wondered where the light switch was, but Emma seemed to have read his mind.

"No lights," she hissed. "Don't you know anything?"

Outside, the footsteps paused, and there was a sudden thump as something hit the door. Again, Joey screamed, but it came out as a loud gasp—still loud enough for Emma to shush him. He moved as far into the room and as far away from the door as he could.

There was a damp, musty smell, like dirty laundry, coming from somewhere, and another smell was beneath it. Rotten food, or rotten *something*.

There was another loud thump on the door, followed by another. Joey took a step backwards and nearly collided with Emma. "What's going on? Who are they? What do they want?"

"They're just ferals," Emma whispered. "Ignore them."

"Ignore them? They attacked me."

"They do that. *Ignore them.*"

Sure enough, the thumps stopped, and Joey heard the sound of shuffling footsteps moving away down the alley.

"I think they've gone," he said, relaxing slightly. There was no answer. "Emma, I said—"

"I heard you," she replied, still whispering.

"It *is* Emma, isn't it?" Joey asked, suddenly wondering if he had made a mistake. "Emma Winrush? Where have you been?"

"Been?" Although Joey couldn't really make out her face, there was no mistaking the sneer in her voice. "I've been *here*. Where else would I have been?"

"But the posters!" Joey protested. "They said you were missing!"

"Keep your voice *down*!" Emma hissed. "They can hear through brick, you idiot!" She paused. "What posters? What are you talking about?"

"There are posters in the newsagent's and everywhere," Joey said, this time dropping his voice to a whisper. "They say you're missing and to call with information. You must have seen them."

"I'm not missing, though, am I?" she said. "I'm here. *Duh*. It's everyone else who's missing, or hadn't you noticed?"

Joey took a second or two to process the information. There was something that didn't add up, not that anything was making sense right now.

"When?" he asked. "When did everyone go missing?"

"It was months ago, wasn't it? Three? I don't know. I lose track. Why? Don't *you* know?"

"It was this morning," Joey said. "For me, anyway."

There was a silence. Even though he could barely see her, he could feel her staring at him.

"You're mad," she said. "I'm not surprised. It's not seeing anyone. I haven't seen anyone for weeks. Apart from Remick, and he comes and goes."

"I'm serious. It was this morning. I was on my way to school to get my results and nearly got hit by a car. Then everyone was gone."

There was another silence.

"Maybe the car did hit me," Joey said eventually. "Maybe I'm dreaming all this."

Emma laughed bitterly. "If I'm your idea of a dream then you really are off your head."

"Who can hear through brick?" Joey asked, to change the subject, and because he suddenly remembered what Emma had said. "You said they could hear through brick. Those men? They've gone, haven't they?"

"Not the ferals. The Screamers. Well, that's what I call them. Remick calls them *Those Bastards*. Jesus, you really don't know, do you? You'll find out in a minute. It's dark enough."

"Screamers? What do you mean?"

"Just shut up for a minute. You'll find out."

"So…you've been living here on your own for months?" Joey couldn't think what else to say. *It would explain the smell. And why you're talking like a lunatic.*

"Here and other places. I get bored if I stay in one place. I stayed at home at first, but it didn't feel right, you know? That house, without my mum there. Not that we got on, but you know what I mean."

Joey got as far as opening his mouth to reply when a shriek ripped through the air outside. It didn't sound quite human. It didn't sound quite like anything Joey had heard before.

"What the hell was *that*?" he gasped.

Emma quickly shushed him, then came closer—so close he could feel her breath on his face and caught the faint smell of cigarettes. "Don't move," she whispered. "Stay still and don't make a sound."

The strange, otherworldly shriek came again, louder and closer this time. It sounded like it was right outside the house. Joey froze. He couldn't have moved even if he'd wanted to. The shriek came again, louder still, and Joey realised he was holding his breath; from the feel of it, so was Emma. He wasn't sure when he'd taken hold of her hand, but her palm was warm and slightly damp in his.

The shrieking sounded like it was right outside the house, and Joey gritted his teeth; it was like biting on tin foil. The shriek vibrated his jaw, invading his mind. Suddenly there was another noise, a lower, male scream. Then there was one more shriek, fainter. Then silence.

"You can let go now," Emma whispered. "It's gone. Sounds like it got your feral friends."

Embarrassed, Joey let go of her hand and stepped away.

"They get you like that," she said, her voice still low. "First time I heard one, I nearly wet myself."

"What *was* that?"

"No idea. Don't think anyone knows. Remick reckons they're the reason everyone's gone. He thinks the Screamers killed everyone and left no trace. He calls them a noise with teeth… among other things."

"Has it…has it killed those men?"

"Probably. Won't leave a trace, though. That's why there's so few of us left. That's what Remick says."

"Who is this Remick?"

"No idea. He just turns up every now and then. When he's sober, he's a good bloke. I just try not to take too much notice of his ideas. There's too much booze lying around for him to keep his head straight."

Joey thought for a minute. "Will the Screamer come back?"

"Sometimes they do. Sometimes they don't. It's like they're searching for something."

"Us?" Joey asked, not really wanting to know the answer.

"Probably," Emma replied. "At least they've had a meal now, so they'll probably leave us alone for tonight. Best thing you can do is try and get some sleep. There are three rooms upstairs. Don't take the first one on the left. That's mine."

"I can't sleep after that!"

"Up to you. Go home if you want, but I wouldn't be going out there again tonight."

"What about you?"

"I need a cig first, then yeah, probably."

Joey fumbled his way to the door of the dark kitchen and opened it. A skylight leaked dim light from outside, and he could make out the stairs to his right. Carefully, he went up onto the landing. Remembering what Emma had said, he ignored the first door he came to and pushed open the one opposite.

He found himself in what appeared to be a small bedroom, though it was hard to tell in the dark. He slowly moved forwards until his shins bumped against something; it turned out to be a single bed. He lay down, inhaling the vague, sweet yet rather sickly perfume, and closed his eyes. His mind held the echo of the terrible shrieks from the Screamer and the cries of the men it had killed. He opened his eyes again, listening to Emma's tread on the stairs. A door opened and closed, and there was the sound of running water. Then that door opened again, and the one opposite Joey's room opened and closed.

Joey listened for a while longer but heard nothing else. He closed his eyes again and this time, quite unexpectedly, fell asleep.

Chapter Seven

JOEY HADN'T EXPECTED to sleep as well as he did. He woke a couple of times, slightly disorientated at being in an unfamiliar room, but fell back to sleep before it could fully register. When he finally woke up properly, morning light was filtering in through curtains he didn't recognise, and he was lying fully clothed in a bed which was facing the wrong way. The room smelled all wrong, too—more like his parents' room, with the lingering odour of the perfume his mother sometimes wore.

With no idea what time it was or how long he'd slept, Joey sat up and automatically reached for the bedside table to look at his alarm clock, but there was no table there. He took in his surroundings, a single bed in a room which was clearly a rarely used spare bedroom, bare of furniture and badly in need of a clean. He tried to process the events of the previous day, but he couldn't. Someone was moving around downstairs; hoping it was Emma, he decided the best thing to do would be to get up and see if she could help him make sense of it all.

He paused briefly to use the toilet, which he found in the bathroom opposite, and threw some water over his face. The towel was damp and smelled like it but he used it anyway, catching a glimpse of himself in the mirror above the sink. For a second, he was looking at a stranger. His dark hair was a mess. It was usually unruly but was now all over the place. His face was pale and tired and a slight stubble—the bane of his dark-haired life since he started shaving—showed on his chin. He looked older, somehow, and not in a good way.

Deciding there was nothing he could do for his face, he took his comb from his back pocket, ran it through his hair and moved away from the mirror. Then he went downstairs to see if the new day had changed anything.

Emma was standing at the back door, smoking and wearing the same clothes as she had the previous day. In the daylight, Joey could see they were all black: a leather jacket, some kind of pullover, leggings and boots. She didn't turn to look when he entered the kitchen, but acknowledged his presence by saying, "About time you got up. Kettle's boiled. There's coffee on the side."

Joey turned the kettle back on and looked on the draining board for a mug. He selected the least stained one and, unable to find a teaspoon, tipped some coffee from the jar—Maxcafé again—into the mug.

"How can you live like this?" he asked, pouring water onto the granules.

"Sorry the house-keeping's not up to scratch," Emma replied sarcastically. "The cleaner never showed up. Anyway, who's to see?"

Joey could not think of a sensible reply, so sipped his coffee in silence.

"When you've had that, you'd better go," Emma said, still not turning around.

"You're getting rid of me?"

"I've been on my own all this time. You get used to it."

"But what am I supposed to do? I don't know what's going on here."

"You survive. That's what I do." She turned to look at him. "Listen, whatever your name is, you'll be better off on your own. Go where you want. *Do* what you want. There's no-one to stop you."

"Joey," he said. "My name's Joey Cale."

"I didn't ask because I don't want to know. We're not going to be mates because when you leave here, we'll never see each other again. You go your way, I'll go mine."

There was a pause in which Emma held Joey's confused gaze briefly, then looked away.

"Do you want another coffee before you go?" she asked.

"I've got my own coffee, thanks." He immediately felt sorry for his petulance.

"Good luck, then," Emma said, turning away and lighting another cigarette.

"You too." Without looking back, Joey went to the front door and left.

Outside on the street, Joey found himself under a grey, overcast sky. Light drizzle hung in the air and settled on his skin, reminding him he had no coat. He shuddered as he glanced down the alley at the side of the house, half expecting to see traces of what had happened to the two tramps the previous night, but there was nothing to see. The best thing he could do was go back to his parents' house—*his* house now—and think about what to do next.

The empty streets were, if anything, more eerie in this miserable weather. He glanced up and down the road, but there was no sign of any 'ferals' as Emma called them, or indeed anyone else. As Joey walked down the road where he had lived all his life, he was aware of the silence, broken only by the echo of his own footsteps. He fished his key out of his pocket and let himself into the house.

It felt even colder than when he'd left it, and he knew without even trying there would be no point calling to his parents. The house was empty, devoid of life, and Joey felt all the more alone for having had some human contact and lost it again. He wanted to cry.

He hung his keys on a hook in the hall and went into the kitchen. Even before he saw it, he knew something was wrong. There was a draught; the back door was very slightly ajar. He remembered going out into the garden the day before, but he was sure he'd closed the door when he came back in. He always did because next door's cat had a tendency to wander in if it could. He was almost certain he'd turned the key, but the bolts…he could not picture himself fastening the bolts.

As he moved cautiously towards the door, his stomach gave a sickening lurch at the crunch under his feet. The floor was covered in shards of glass. Someone had smashed the panel in the door and broken into the house. Joey didn't have time to curse himself for leaving the key in the lock before the horrifying realisation washed over him…*they might still be here.* Maybe the two men who had attacked him had got away somehow, or maybe they weren't the only ones.

His instinct was to get out of the house fast and get help, but unless everyone had suddenly come back, there was no-one to call. Instead, he grabbed a carving knife from the block by the cooker and cautiously retraced his steps, back out to the hall, pausing by the kitchen door to listen, but he could hear no sound.

Moving as quietly as he could, he crept into the living room. Nothing in there had been disturbed. The television, sofa, chairs—everything was just as he had left it. He returned to the hall and glanced into the front room—a room only used by his parents if they wanted a bit of peace and quiet to read, or if his mother wanted to play the old upright piano they had inherited from her parents. Again, there was no sign anything had been disturbed. *Upstairs, then.*

Holding the knife out in front of him, Joey climbed the stairs, one at a time, listening as he did so. The second-to-last stair creaked. It always had, but this time, it sounded so loud he paused, his heart pounding. But the creak was the only sound in the house.

At the top of the stairs, Joey looked into the bathroom, then through the open door of the spare bedroom, which his parents used as a box room because no-one ever came to stay. Nothing. With trepidation, he pushed open the door of his parents' bedroom, expecting to see drawers and wardrobes open as the intruder hunted for jewellery maybe, but the room showed no signs of anyone having been in there since his parents were last there. That left only one room: Joey's.

Joey kept his bedroom door closed. It wasn't that he had any particular need for privacy, but he didn't tidy up as often as he should and didn't want his mum doing it for him because he could never find anything afterwards. The door stuck a bit—something his dad was always meaning to sort out but never got around to—

but right now, it was half open. Joey racked his brains, trying to remember if he had closed it the previous morning or if he had been in too much of a hurry to get his results. He didn't know.

Taking a deep breath, he pushed the door open as hard as he could so that it banged against the wall, startling any intruders. But there was nobody in there to startle. Whoever had been in the house had gone.

As Joey looked around at the wreckage of his room, at the open drawers of his desk and their contents strewn all over the floor and the bed, he felt a fury rising in him. Whoever had been in here had come for only one purpose: to search *his* room. There was only *one* person that could be; only one person who knew he even existed. There was, in fact, apart from the two ferals, only one person around at all.

He sat down on one of the few clear spaces on his bed, seething. He tried to come up with another explanation, but it kept coming back to one thing and one person. He knew then he had to do something about it.

Joey flew down the stairs, grabbed his keys and stormed out of the house. He ran full pelt down the road and rounded the corner into Bridge Street. Flinging open the front door of the house he had only recently left, he marched through to the kitchen only then realising he was still carrying the knife.

That, and the noise he had made on his way in, probably explained the look of shock on Emma's face as she shot up from where she had been sitting at the kitchen table, a plate of sandwiches in front of her. Her chair toppled with a crash, and she backed away, glancing behind her at the open door.

"Okay," Joey said, still breathing hard from running. "Do you want to tell me what the hell you were doing in my house?"

Chapter Eight

I HAVEN'T BEEN IN your house." Emma paused too long and her voice wavered too much for Joey not to be able to tell instantly she was lying. "Maybe those ferals weren't alone."

"Why my house and not one of the others? There isn't anyone else. There's nobody else *here*. So, come on. What were you looking for? And how the hell did you even know where I live?"

"Put the knife away." Emma had regained some of her composure. "You'll cut yourself."

Joey didn't move. "Tell me," he demanded, sounding harder than he felt.

"Put the knife down first," Emma challenged.

Joey hesitated, then put the knife down on the kitchen table.

"Sit down," Emma said, picking up her chair. "And for God's sake, calm down."

Still, Joey stayed where he was. "You broke into my house. You smashed the glass and broke in. You turned my room upside down. Everyone I know has vanished and I'm stuck here with you, a bunch of psycho tramps and that…that Screamer thing that eats people, and you're telling me to calm down? Are you bloody stupid or something?"

"No need to swear," Emma said calmly. "It sounds all wrong coming from you. Come on. Sit down."

Reluctantly, Joey joined her at the table but he kept his eyes on the knife. There was a long pause, then Emma sighed.

"There are other people around," she said. "At least, I think so. Not just ferals but other people. I've never seen them, but you see signs. It wasn't hard to know where you live, though. I saw you come out of the house and start banging on people's doors."

"Why did you break in? What were you looking for?"

"You won't like it."

"I don't like it now. You had no right."

"The rules are different now. I'm used to going where I want when I want. There's no-one to stop me. I told you, I do what I do to survive."

"Like breaking into houses. But why mine?"

"Because you made me think. You showing up has changed everything. I needed to find out who you are." Emma reached for her cigarettes which were on the table, then stopped. "Mind if I smoke?" she asked.

"It's your house."

"No, it isn't. Not really. I just stay here." She lit a cigarette and took a long drag on it, blowing the smoke out slowly. "I never used to. Smoke, I mean. Well, only sometimes. I do it out of boredom now."

"It'll kill you," Joey said.

"Who'd notice?"

"So…what have I changed? What's so important about me that you had to break into my house? You could have just asked."

"Remick is the only person I've actually spoken to since everyone else disappeared. Then you showed up. But you said it had only just happened."

"It had," Joey said. "Yesterday."

"But not for me," said Emma. "It happened ages ago. I've been on my own for months. It's hard to keep track, but everyone else vanished months ago. That's what made me think. And you said I'd been on posters."

"You were. There was one in the newsagent's for ages."

"Don't you see? That changes *everything*. Everyone else—they haven't disappeared. We have."

Joey stared at her.

"But we're here," he said. He was about to argue further, but then he remembered. *Different newsagent's. Different Doctor Who...* "Different President," he finished out loud.

Emma raised an eyebrow.

"I saw a newspaper. The president isn't Trump. It's some guy called Irving. And the coffee isn't right."

"What's coffee got to do with it? Tastes okay to me."

"Look at the jar," Joey suggested.

Emma picked up the coffee jar, glanced at it and put it down again. "It's coffee," she said.

"Have you ever seen that brand before?"

"This isn't my house, remember?"

"Doesn't matter." Joey was getting exasperated. "You don't notice much, do you? I've never seen this coffee before. There's a different president. Even the newsagent up the road is a different shop, and it doesn't have your poster in it. You're right, Emma. This isn't our world. We're somewhere else."

Emma took off her leather jacket and sat down at the table. She looked at her cigarette packet but seemed to change her mind.

"There's something you need to see," she said and rolled her sleeve up.

Chapter Nine

A T FIRST, JOEY couldn't see why Emma had rolled up her sleeve. Other than being slightly grubby, her bare arm looked normal, but then she twisted it and showed him the underside. Beneath the thin layer of grime, he could make out fine scars which criss-crossed her skin.

Emma looked up, trying to read Joey's face. "Aren't you going to say something?"

"You really need a shower."

"Funny," Emma said but didn't laugh.

"Did you do that?" Joey asked.

"Yes. Of course I did. And?" Her face had a defiance in it like she was expecting an argument.

"And nothing. A girl in my year did the same. Ciara Wright. She got counselling."

"Aren't you going to ask me why I do it?"

"None of my business. Why did you show me?"

Emma took a deep breath. "Because it's something else that's different. I haven't done it since…well, since whatever happened, happened. Haven't wanted to."

"I don't get it," Joey said.

"You're not a cutter, though, are you? I bet you've never even thought about it. I bet you're a good boy who never does anything wrong."

"So what?" Joey snapped. "Just because I don't…do *that*…"

"Cut myself," Emma said. "It's okay to say it, you know. It's not catching."

"God, you're defensive. I wasn't attacking you. What you do is your business."

"Yeah, that's kind of what my mum thought," Emma replied sullenly. "That's why I did it."

"Why are you showing me?" Joey asked again. "What do you want me to say?"

"Because it doesn't matter why I did it. I don't want to do it any more. Most of the time, I don't even think about it, and I used to think about it all the time. The only time I think about it now is when they itch."

"Itch? I don't—"

"The scars itch," Emma replied. "They never used to. Only when they were first healing, but that was a different itch. Now, they itch at night."

For the first time, Joey saw something in Emma's eyes other than the grim defiance that had been there since he met her. For the first time, he saw something like fear.

"They itch when the Screamers are coming," she said. "That's how I know."

Joey looked from Emma's face to her arm, then back again.

"Why do they do that?" she asked. "It's like they know. How do they do that?"

"I don't know," Joey said simply. "I'm not sure I know anything."

"Anyway," Emma tugged her sleeve down and stood up, "you're right. I need a shower. I'm minging."

"Right," Joey said, turning to the door. "I'll just…"

"I won't be long," she replied, then hesitated. "You could stay. Have a weird coffee or something."

"Okay," he agreed.

With a quick smile, Emma brushed past him and went into the hall. He listened as her footsteps hurried up the stairs, then filled the kettle and ran some hot water into the sink to wash one of the mugs which had been abandoned there. Almost as an afterthought, he washed a second and hunted around for a tea towel. One had been tossed onto the work surface, and it was crumpled but reasonably clean. He shook it out and dried the two mugs, but as he turned to pick up the coffee jar, he caught sight of what was on the table.

"You brought a knife," he said to himself. "You bloody idiot."

He quickly grabbed the knife and put it away in a drawer. From upstairs, he could hear the sound of the shower running. Suddenly he felt the same sense of dislocation he'd felt when he started to notice the changes, like the coffee, like the president. There was something else nagging at the back of his mind, and he couldn't quite put his finger on it. It was only when the kettle finished boiling and clicked itself off that he realised what it was.

There's power. There's power and water. If all the people are gone, how is that happening? And the food...

He needed something to write on. Hunting around the kitchen, he found a pile of discarded mail, within which was a large white junk-mail envelope. A pen had been tossed onto the work surface nearby. He sat at the table and began to make a list, so absorbed in writing, he barely noticed Emma come into the kitchen behind him, towel-drying her wet hair.

"What are you up to?" she asked.

"Making a list—a list of things that don't make sense."

"*You* don't make sense," she said, but for once, she did it without sounding snide.

"Okay." Joey put his pen down. "Actually, *nothing* makes sense. Too many things depend on people. How is the power on? Why is there food around? Where do *you* get food from?"

"I just take it from the shops. There's no-one to stop me."

"How is it even there, though?" Joey indicated the sandwiches which Emma had abandoned earlier. "You've been here months. No-one delivers the food to the shops. Why isn't it rotten? Why hasn't it run out?"

Emma sat down opposite him. "I hadn't thought about that."

Talking about food made Joey realise he was hungry. He had no real idea of what time it was, or when he'd last eaten.

Emma saw him eyeing up the sandwiches. "Go ahead," she invited.

Joey took a sandwich and bit into it. "Think about this, then," he said. "This is the big one. If all the people disappeared from here—wherever here is—and they all disappeared at the same time, lots of them must have been driving cars. Why aren't there crashed cars everywhere? The cars are just there, in the middle of the road. They couldn't park themselves, and there's no way everyone stopped and got out. Not all at the same time. And planes. What about planes? If all the people just vanished, it should be like the end of the world out there. But it isn't. Why not?"

"The Screamers took them. Like those two last night."

"But it's the same thing. Imagine if one of those things attacked you while you were driving. They're not going to politely ask you to pull over, are they?"

There was silence while they both mulled it over.

Eventually, Emma asked, "If all the people didn't just vanish, and the Screamers didn't get them, where are they?"

"I think I can answer that," a voice said from the hall, making them both jump. Joey turned in his chair to see an older man standing there. The man was nearly as dishevelled as the two tramps, and for one horrible second, Joey thought they'd come back. But this stranger, although he had the same uncut hair and scraggly beard, was wearing a leather jacket—which looked like it had been run over by a bus—and jeans. Very battered jeans.

"Remick," Emma greeted him. "I wondered when you'd show up again."

Chapter Ten

REMICK CAME IN without being invited and without acknowledging Joey further. He hung his scabby leather jacket on the back of the chair and sat down. "Kettle on, Em?"

Emma surprised Joey by getting up meekly, with no sarcastic remarks, and switching the kettle back on. There was silence while it boiled and Emma made Remick's coffee. It was only when his coffee was placed in front of him, and Emma had sat down, that Remick looked at Joey again.

"I was wondering when you'd get here," he said.

"How do you mean?" Joey was confused.

"Em's been on her own too long. I think things will start now you're here."

"Start? What things?"

"Things. I'm not sure. I guess we'll find out."

"I'm sorry, Mr. Remick, but I don't know what you're talking about."

"Neither do I," Remick said. "Not really. That's the problem with the visions you get when you're drunk. They're a bit—you know—fuzzy. And it's just Remick. Forget the Mister."

"Remick sees stuff," Emma explained. "Usually when he's drunk."

"I'm not surprised," Joey said.

"Not that sort of stuff." Emma scowled at him. "Visions. That kind of thing. He says he knew I was going to be here before he saw me."

"Trouble is, I don't seem to be able to stay drunk long enough to make sense of it," Remick said and laughed a throaty, moist laugh. "I do try."

"What's that got to do with me?" Joey wanted to know.

"I knew you were coming before you showed up. I'd sunk a bottle of Jack Daniel's and I saw you. There's something about you, lad. Something to do with—your heart, is it?"

"I was born with a hole in my heart," Joey said. "It's okay now."

Remick nodded. "That's not what I saw. It's kind of hard to explain. I saw you and there was...well, the best way to describe it is like a light coming from your chest." He noticed Emma was about to protest and held a hand up to silence her. "Yeah, I know. But I'm just saying what I saw. I don't control these things, you know."

"So, what?" Joey asked. "What does it mean?"

"I don't have a clue," Remick answered with a laugh Joey didn't like very much. "Like I say, I only get the visions. I don't know what they mean. I've been waiting for you to arrive to find out. The thing is, you can't stay here."

"What? Why not?"

"Because it wasn't here I saw you. You were in, like, a field or something. I don't know. It wasn't clear. I think there were other people there too."

There was silence for a moment, and then Emma said, "Right. Let's get this straight. Joey's important for some reason but you don't know why. It's something to do with his heart but you don't know what. And he has to go and stand in a field and you don't know where. Remick, you're bloody useless."

"Look, I don't—"

"—control the visions. I know. You said."

"You also said you might know where everyone's gone," Joey pointed out, to change the subject.

"Yeah. I think you're right. I don't think they have gone anywhere. I think they're right where you left them when you came here."

"No," Emma said firmly. "I don't get it. I know this place. This is Waterloo. I've lived round here all my life. It's exactly the same only no people."

"But it's *not* exactly the same," Remick argued. "Your mate here has noticed the differences."

"Joey. My name is—"

Remick talked over him. "It's like Waterloo, but it isn't your Waterloo."

"All that booze has wrecked your bloody head," Emma said. "You've lost it." She and Remick glared at each other while Joey stared at them both. For the first time since he'd come 'here', he was conscious of the sound of his heart's steady beat, and how it had felt like it stopped when he thought the car was going to hit him.

"I thought I'd died," he said. Emma and Remick stopped trying to stare each other out and looked at him instead. "I thought I'd been hit by a car and my heart stopped. And then I was here. I thought maybe I was dreaming all this."

Emma frowned. "Well, you're not."

"Red King," Remick said. Seeing the blank looks he was getting, he went on. "Don't you know your *Alice in Wonderland*?"

"Saw the film," Emma said. "It was crap."

"That's why you should read books," Remick replied. "In Wonderland, they thought the Red King was asleep and dreaming all their lives so they couldn't wake him up or their lives would end."

"So you do think I'm dreaming this?" Joey asked.

"No, I don't. I think it's just a story. This is real, but it isn't bloody Wonderland. But if your heart has something to do with getting you here, maybe it can get you back."

"How?"

"I don't know." Remick shrugged. "I might need another vision to find out."

"Well, you'd better have one fast," Emma said, and Joey noticed she was scratching her arms, first one and then the other, her bitten nails leaving red welts on her skin. "I think something's coming."

"We'd better not waste any time, then." Remick grinned. "Emma, you got anything to drink in this place?"

Chapter Eleven

EMMA DIDN'T HAVE any alcohol in the house, as it turned out, so Remick went back out to find some. He was gone for nearly an hour. During that time, Joey and Emma barely spoke to each other. Emma paced up and down, rubbing her arms and watching out of the window for Remick and looking at the sky as it began to grow darker. Joey couldn't help but feel the dusk was coming far earlier than it should for August.

When Remick finally returned, offering no explanation as to why he had been away so long, Emma rinsed out a glass and placed it in front of him. Remick opened a bottle and filled the glass. Then they all sat down to watch him drink.

There was, Joey thought, not much that was more depressing than watching someone deliberately trying to get drunk. It reminded him of his Uncle Brian drinking glass after glass of wine at Christmas—much to his Aunty Lynda's embarrassment—and roaring out jokes that only he found funny until he fell asleep, snoring in an armchair. Brian and Lynda had moved away to Knutsford five years ago and didn't come for Christmas any more.

As Remick topped up his glass again, there was none of Brian's forced jollity. If anything, he seemed to sink lower and lower into gloom the more he drank.

"I don't even like the stuff," he said at one point, taking another large gulp. "Didn't touch it till…" He stopped without explaining further.

He was three-quarters of the way through the bottle, his face getting redder and his eyes becoming more and more watery, before he suddenly tensed and dropped his glass on the table, spilling its remaining contents. Joey made a move to help him, but Emma held him back.

"Leave him," she said in a low voice. "It's starting."

Joey thought Remick was going to have a fit, like Chris Metcalfe in his school who was epileptic and would suddenly tense up and then drop to the classroom floor or playground. Remick sat rigid in his chair, gripping the edges of the table so hard it looked like he was trying to break it. His mouth moved as if he was speaking, but only incoherent sounds came out.

Emma sat scratching her arms and muttering, "Come on, come on!" with her head cocked to one side, listening. Then Joey heard what she had been listening for, in the distance, like the rumbling noise from the docks he sometimes heard on a clear night, except this was an unmistakable eerie, blood-chilling shriek. But it was different to the noise the Screamer had made the previous night. This time, there were several shrieks, all wound around each other in hideous discord.

"There's more than one!" Emma hissed, terror in her eyes for the first time since Joey had met her. "Oh shit!" she gasped. "The door! Did he shut the door?"

Emma moved to get up, but Joey beat her to it and rushed into the hall. The front door was wide open, a strong draught coming through it. The shrieks were getting closer, tearing the air apart from all sides, and Joey had to force his feet to move to get to the door, his every instinct telling him to run in the opposite direction. But he kept moving forward and had his hand on the door, pushing it shut as the shrieks reached a crescendo and something forced the door back against him. There was something out there that he couldn't quite see, something made of hate and teeth trying to stop him closing the door.

He got his shoulder against it, but the shrieks filled his ears and his head, and he could barely think let alone push. His body felt chilled to the marrow of his bones, as if something was tugging at his skin. He was on the verge of letting go and just going with it to make the feeling stop when he felt a *thud* in his chest like a small detonation. His head filled with a dazzling white light, and for a second, that was all he knew. No feeling, no noise, just light. That second was all he needed to slam the door shut. He dropped to his knees in the hall, spent of all strength and emotion as the shrieks circled the house and then, finally, retreated.

He was only dimly aware of Emma by his side, crouching and trying to pull him to his feet.

"Come on," she was saying. "They've gone. How did you *do* that?"

"Don't know," Joey mumbled.

His legs felt like jelly, but somehow he hauled himself to his feet and let Emma lead him back into the kitchen. She sat him down in a chair and thrust a glass into his hand. Joey automatically took a sip and then choked when the whiskey burned the back of his throat. He put the glass down and tried to clear his head. He was in the kitchen, sitting at the table. Emma hovered close by while Remick was slumped over the table, his head on his arms, apparently asleep. He did not know what had happened, but he was back. He felt like he wanted to sleep forever, but he was alive.

"You beat them," Emma said, looking at him with something close to wonder. "You actually beat them! How…?"

"I don't know," Joey replied, clearer this time, but his voice was hoarse and felt like it didn't quite belong to him. "My heart…it did something…the light…I don't know."

"Did you see them? What are they like?"

"You don't see them." Joey tried to remember. "It's like…I don't know what to call it. It's like they're not quite there. You don't *want* to see them. I don't think your brain can cope." He waved a hand to indicate Remick, only his rough breathing giving any impression that he was still alive. "What happened to him?"

"I don't know. He was sitting up when I went to help you, and when I came back he was like that."

"Keep the noise down," Remick said, his voice muffled by his arm. "Christ, I've got a bad head."

"Did you see anything?" Emma demanded. "Remick, what did you see?"

"Coffee. Then you need to start packing. You're going on a road trip."

Chapter Twelve

JOEY AND EMMA had been walking for nearly an hour before the absurdity of the situation really began to sink in. Remick's vision had been similar to the one he'd experienced earlier—Joey in a field, light coming out of his chest, other people around—but there were two significant differences. One: Emma was there but Remick was not; two: the shape in the background was distinct, and Remick had recognised it immediately.

"Are you sure it was Pendle Hill?" Emma asked. "Not just a hill?"

"I know Pendle," Remick replied. "I've spent plenty of nights there." He didn't elaborate any further, and neither Joey nor Emma seemed inclined to ask.

So that seemed to settle it. Joey and Emma were to head for Pendle Hill and see what happened. Emma suggested going by car, seeing as there were plenty of them around and she'd taken a few driving lessons. However, as Remick pointed out, if there were cars stalled on the roads around Waterloo, the chances were it would be the same everywhere else and some roads would be rendered impassable. For reasons he did not make clear, he also rejected the idea of bikes or motorbikes. It would, he said, have to be on foot.

So, after a fitful night's sleep and a hasty breakfast, Emma had packed a bag and then she and Remick had escorted Joey back to his house where he did the same. There was no need to take any supplies, they decided, as there would be plenty of places to pick up everything they would need on the way. Remick waved them off and they'd started walking.

As they left Waterloo, Joey glanced back and out of the corner of his eye caught Emma doing the same. Neither of them said anything, but both had the same thought, a nagging doubt that they might ever come back.

They walked in silence at first. Every road was lined with empty, immobile cars, and Joey noticed for the first time—*really* noticed—that as well as no people, there were no other signs of life. There were always cats wandering the streets of Waterloo—at least two in Joey's own road—but they saw none. The silence which surrounded them felt even more unnatural because of the lack of birdsong. There were so many sounds he had taken for granted until they were no longer there. It made conversation seem unnecessary, even intrusive, so they walked quietly, concentrating on putting one foot in front of the other.

A change seemed to have come over Emma, too, and it was more than a reaction to the lack of noise around them. She seemed to have withdrawn into herself, taking no notice of her surroundings, just staring at the ground and walking almost with a determination *not* to communicate.

They had walked maybe four or five miles before the silence became intolerable and Joey spoke.

"All this because of a vision. It could be a waste of time."

Emma didn't reply, just kept walking.

"Emma," Joey said, then repeated firmly, "*Emma.*"

This time, she stopped and turned to him. "What?" she asked, exasperation in her voice. "God!"

"I said this is probably a waste of time. What's up with you? You've not said a word since we left."

"I don't like change, all right? I was okay there."

"Then let's get it done and go back. If there's anything there."

Emma stepped off, once again appearing to be taking no notice. Joey decided not to press it.

"Don't you believe him?" she asked, eventually.

"The man has visions when he's off his face on whiskey, so we're walking to Pendle." Joey shrugged and looked at Emma, who raised an eyebrow.

"I don't know. Maybe. It's just…I don't get any of this. I don't know what we're going *for*. You don't want to go and I don't feel like walking all the way to Pendle for nothing. So why are we?"

"Remick seemed to think it was important. He seemed to think we might find the answers. You might find the way home."

"*We* might, you mean."

"Yeah, whatever."

"And you believe him. Why? He seems a nutcase to me. Why do you believe what he says?"

"I don't know. It's like… It's like the madness is all an act. I think he knows stuff. And if he reckons he can get you home—"

"What about you? Don't you miss home?" Joey tried not to think about how much he did.

"Maybe. Not much difference, really. I was on my own there. I'm on my own here."

"Why didn't he come with us?" Joey asked. "Remick, I mean. If it's so important, why has he stayed behind?"

"He told us. He said he wasn't there in the vision."

"Yes but it was *his* vision. If you take a photograph, you're not in the photo, are you? Unless it's a selfie. It seems a bit convenient to me. He gets rid of us and stays behind."

"We'll find out when we get there," Emma said.

"Or not."

"Yes, or not."

They lapsed back into silence and walked on, trudging along the side of the main road to Ormskirk, a road normally busy with traffic, but now still and frozen. Joey wondered again why Emma was so quick to believe Remick when she didn't seem to trust anything. It was like Remick had some kind of hold over her and she wouldn't hear a word against him. Did she fancy him or something? The thought made Joey feel strangely jealous. But there had certainly been a change in Emma. When he'd first met her—was it really only two days ago?—she had seemed so self-reliant, so sure that she needed nothing and nobody. Now, on the word of a weird piss-head, she was happy to leave everything behind. Even if they kept going and didn't stop to rest, it would take a day or two to reach Pendle Hill. If they didn't start talking again soon, it was going to be a very long journey.

They had been walking for another half an hour or so when, to his horror, Joey saw movement on the other side of the main road. Concealed behind a hedge, he could see the shape of a person. Somebody was there, ducking behind the bushes and following the same route they were.

Chapter Thirteen

JOEY TRIED TO get Emma's attention by nudging her. She shot him an irritated look, like *grow up*, but he nudged her again and indicated the other side of the road. He tried to do it casually without breaking his stride. At first, Emma still didn't know what he meant, but then the figure on the other side of the road appeared briefly in a gap between two bushes, and she saw.

"They're following us," she whispered, aware her voice would carry in the silence.

"Let's stop," Joey suggested. "See if they carry on."

"You're right," Emma said loudly so that she could be heard. "I could do with a rest."

With that, she put her bag on the grass verge and sat on it. Joey did the same. They both tried to look like they weren't watching whoever it was. Emma dug out a bottle of water she had acquired from a petrol station they'd passed. She took a long swig from it and offered it to Joey. He drank some, glancing from time to time at the bushes. For a while, there was no movement, but then suddenly, before he could stop her, Emma was on her feet and sprinting across the road, swerving her way around the stationary cars.

Joey swore to himself, then grabbed both their belongings and followed, the bags banging against his legs as he ran. Even though, at the back of his mind, he knew the cars weren't moving, he still felt anxious as he ran between them, as if they would suddenly spring into action. When he reached the other side, he heard a commotion from behind the bushes and, pushing his way through the foliage, saw Emma squatting on the ground with a figure pinned beneath her. Whoever it was had their arms across their face to shield themselves while Emma rained down slaps on them.

"I said, '*Why are you following us?*' you little shitbag. Answer me!"

The figure just made whimpering noises by way of reply, and Joey realised it was just a young kid, a blonde-haired boy, maybe ten or so. Joey dropped the bags and grabbed Emma from behind, trying to drag her off the prone figure underneath her. Emma struggled like a cat, her attention now on Joey.

"Get *off*!" she snarled and aimed a bite at Joey's hand. He snatched it away just in time, and as Emma struggled against him, the person she'd been holding down managed to squirm free.

A well-placed elbow from Emma smashed into Joey's nose, and he fell over backwards.

"Jesus, Joey, what are you doing?" she demanded, turning on him.

"He's just a kid!" he answered angrily, feeling blood running from his nose into his mouth. "You've broken my nose, you mad cow!" He turned his back on Emma and spoke to the boy. "It's okay. We won't hurt you."

"She's psycho!"

"Yes, I know." That earned Joey another filthy scowl from Emma. "But she's all right. We just want to know why you were following us."

"I wasn't!" the boy protested. "I thought you were following *me*. I thought you were more of the bad people."

"You don't know the half of it," Emma muttered. Joey shot her a look, and she turned away, arms folded over her chest.

"What bad people?" he asked.

"The ones who tried to catch me and Ruby. But we got away."

"Who's Ruby?"

"She's my sister. I left her at the barn while I came out to get some food, and then I saw you. Then *she* attacked me."

"We're not bad people," Joey said. "We're just passing through on our way…somewhere. I'm Joey and this is Emma."

"I'm Evan." The boy took a tentative step closer. He looked at Joey, frowning, then his eyes opened wide with surprise. "You're *him*!" he gasped.

"What?" Joey asked. "Who?"

"You're the Light Man! I've dreamed about you! So has Ruby!" The boy, Evan, was suddenly animated and excited, all fear gone. "This is brilliant! You've got to come and meet Rubes! She's not gonna believe this!"

"No, listen—" Joey began but Emma interrupted him.

"A word," she said, beckoning him over.

Joey gave Evan an apologetic glance and went to Emma, who grabbed him by the arm and led him further away.

"What the hell do you think you're doing?" she asked, keeping her voice low. "We need to get moving."

"We can't just leave them!" Joey replied. "They're kids."

"They're not our problem, *Light Man*," She made no effort to disguise her sarcasm. "We need to keep moving. We've got a long way to go, and I don't want to be slowed down by babysitting."

"Then you go on," Joey snapped. "If you only care about yourself, then you go on. I want to make sure these kids are okay and then I might catch you up."

"Remick said we had to go together."

"Yeah, because of a vision he had when he was pissed. These kids are on their own. That's real. I'm not leaving here until I know they're okay."

Emma stared at him for a moment, then threw her hands up in frustration. "Fine!" she said. "An hour. Then I'm going on with or without you." She paused. "How's the nose?"

"Okay." Joey touched it and winced. It was still throbbing, but there was no fresh blood. Not broken, then. "It's stopped bleeding."

He waited for an apology, soon realising the fact she'd asked at all was as close as he was going to get.

"Come on, then," he said to Evan. "You want to show us this barn and let us meet Ruby?"

"Is *she* coming?" Evan asked hesitantly. "Your girlfriend?"

Joey and Emma both spoke at the same time.

"She's not!"

"I'm not!"

"She won't do anything else to hurt you," Joey finished.

Evan considered this and then said, "It's this way," and headed off across the field, with Joey and a still sullen Emma following behind.

Chapter Fourteen

THE BARN PROVED to be part of a farm several fields away. Joey walked alongside Evan, with Emma still hanging back a bit, and Evan told Joey some of his story.

Evan and Ruby were brother and sister. Evan was eleven, Ruby a year younger. They had found themselves alone in Formby, several miles away; Evan was not particularly clear about how long ago, but Joey got the impression it was weeks rather than days. They had stayed in the house where they lived with their mother and stepfather, fending for themselves, waiting for someone to come, but no-one did. Eventually, they decided to go and try to find someone—anyone. Just outside Formby, they had gone into a large Tesco to get some supplies when they came across three adults—two men and a woman—who were stealing televisions and mobile phones.

Evan and Ruby had run out of the store with the three thieves in hot pursuit, but when they'd reached the car park, the looters had stopped dead, looking around. For some reason, they seemed unable to see Evan and Ruby, even though at one point they looked right at them. Evan and Ruby ran without looking back and kept going. They had found the barn two nights earlier and sheltered there.

"Why the barn?" Joey asked. "You said it was part of a farm. Couldn't you stay in the farmhouse?"

"Yeah, well, that's like someone else's house, isn't it?" Evan answered. "It isn't right."

Joey couldn't argue with the logic. What wasn't right was that two young kids were forced to look after themselves. But then, there were plenty of things that weren't right these days.

Before he could ask any more questions, they arrived at the farm. It had a sizeable farmhouse, with a variety of barns and outbuildings, and looked like it had been a large operation. Now, it was as deserted as everywhere else. There were no animals in the barns or fields, and a tractor and a mud-covered Land Rover sat silent in the yard.

Evan stopped outside one of the barns. "I'll just tell Ruby we're here. I don't want to scare her." He went in, leaving Joey and Emma outside.

"He seems a good kid," Joey said, trying to make conversation.

"An hour," Emma replied grimly.

Soon after, Evan emerged from the barn, and at first, Joey thought he was on his own, but then he saw a blonde-haired girl was hiding behind him. If she was indeed ten, she looked small for her age. Shyly, she stepped forward and Joey noticed she was clutching an old, very battered stuffed badger.

"See?" Evan said. "It *is* him!"

Without warning, Ruby ran to Joey and hugged him tightly. Joey looked over Ruby's head at Emma, who shrugged, her mouth a hard line. *I don't care how much she hugs you*, the look said, *they're not coming*. But then Ruby broke away from Joey and threw her arms around Emma.

"I knew you'd come too," she said in a tiny voice, muffled by Emma's jumper. "You're the lady who knows."

"Knows what?" Emma extricated herself from the little girl's embrace.

"You know when the noise is coming. The noise with teeth. It's your arms."

"How do you know that?" Emma demanded, seizing Ruby by the shoulders. "How do you *know*?"

"I dreamed it," Ruby said simply.

Emma let Ruby go and walked away a few paces. "Oookay. This is officially freaking me out now. I mean what the f… What the hell is going on here?"

"Let's go inside and talk about it," Joey suggested. "Maybe have something to eat. You hungry, guys?" Evan and Ruby both nodded. "Let's go and see your barn, then."

The barn was half full of hay bales, stacked nearly to the roof, and Joey could see a couple of coats laid out where Evan and Ruby had clearly nested for the night. There was a chill in the air inside, and dust and fragments of hay drifted in the shafts of light which broke through gaps in the walls.

"Place is probably swarming with rats," Emma said to no-one in particular.

"Come on, guys." Joey carried his bag over to one of the hay bales and sat down. "I know I've got some biscuits in here." He opened his bag and rooted around. "Emma, have we got any of those butties left?"

Emma sighed and sat down on a nearby bale. Soon, she too had opened her bag, and the four of them were tucking into an improvised picnic.

"So, tell us about these dreams," Joey said, his mouth full of sandwich. "When did you start having them?"

Ruby looked to Evan, who answered.

"Just the last couple of nights. After we left Formby."

"And what are the dreams like?"

"They're funny dreams." Evan frowned as he tried to remember. "You're there, in this field, and there's this light…I don't know. It's like white and dead bright."

"And you're there," Ruby said to Emma. "I saw that, but Evan didn't. You're like holding your arms because something bad is coming."

"What else did you see?" Emma asked, interested despite herself.

"That's it," Evan said. "That's all we could remember. There were some other people there, but I don't know who they are."

"And the bad burning thing," Ruby murmured fearfully.

"What bad thing?" Joey asked, but Ruby shook her head and clutched her badger tightly to her face. She looked like she might be about to cry. "It's okay." Joey put his arm around the girl. "You can tell us."

"I don't know," Ruby said, her voice little more than a whisper.

"What's the bad thing, Evan?" Joey asked again. "Do you know?"

"I don't know. She says it's like…like a man but it isn't, and he's on fire. I don't know."

"It's okay. Dreams are like that."

They carried on eating a while longer. Then suddenly, and without a word, Emma stood up and walked out of the barn. Joey told the kids he would be back in a minute and followed her outside. She was standing in the yard smoking—the first time Joey had seen her smoke since they'd left Waterloo.

"Don't want to set light to the place," she said.

"I know what you're thinking," Joey began.

"I doubt it."

"They've got to come with us. You heard them. Their dreams are just like Remick's vision. They're part of this too. I don't know how, but it's all connected."

"No."

"We can't just leave them!"

"No!" Emma dropped her cigarette on the floor and ground it out. "We can't look after them. I'm not going to be responsible for a couple of kids."

"They haven't got anyone else!"

"I can't do it, Joey." For the first time since they had met, Joey could see tears forming in her eyes. "I can't even be responsible for myself. I'll let them down."

Joey put his arms round her; it felt right to do so. He could feel her face resting against his shoulder, feel her breathe. "I don't think we have any choice," he said.

Chapter Fifteen

IT TOOK RATHER longer than Joey had expected to get Evan and Ruby organised to leave. He'd thought it would just be a question of them gathering their things and then hitting the road, but it proved to be a bit more complicated than that. The main problem was that Ruby refused to go.

"We've got to go," Evan protested. "It's just like the dream."

Joey heard Emma mutter, "No, it's fine," from somewhere behind him and knew he had to act quickly to stop the whole situation from running out of control. He couldn't leave Evan and Ruby on their own; nor could he and Emma stay.

He sat on a hay bale next to Ruby, who was cowering back against a wall. "You can't stay here, Ruby," he said gently. "It isn't safe."

"I don't want to go." Tears spilled down Ruby's cheeks. "I don't want to."

"You'll be safe with me and Emma. We'll look after you."

"I don't want to," Ruby cried again. It looked like a full-on storm was brewing.

"If she doesn't want to, she doesn't want to," Emma said. Joey ignored her.

"Come on, Rubes," Evan implored, joining Joey on the bale. "They'll look after you. What if those people at Tesco come after us?"

Ruby looked at Evan, and then at Joey.

"I think she wants to talk to me," Evan said.

Joey got up and walked over to where Emma was waiting while Ruby whispered to Evan, glancing up from time to time to make sure no-one was listening.

"It's a wonderful thing you're doing," Emma said; Joey wasn't sure if she was being sarcastic. "But we're wasting time."

"What time?" Joey asked, feeling pretty sarcastic himself. "Nobody told me we had a deadline."

"Whoa! Chill out a minute. *No*, we haven't got a deadline. Not as far as I know. But we need to get a move on before it starts getting dark. Do you want to be outside if there are Screamers round here?"

"I can handle them," Joey said, sounding more confident than he felt.

"You handled them *once*. We need to get further down the road and then find somewhere safe."

"If there are Screamers round here, they'll get the kids," Joey said. "I'm not going to let that happen."

"Then you'd better convince Princess Ruby. But do it fast."

They were interrupted by Evan tugging at Joey's coat.

"She says she doesn't want to go because Mum might come back and won't be able to find us."

"That's stupid!" Emma snapped. "They're not coming back. They're not even here!"

It was Evan's turn to start welling up, and Joey felt completely out of his depth. Maybe Emma was right.

"Listen, Evan," he said, "we've worked out what's happened. Your mum and dad are still there, back in Formby. But somehow this isn't the world we know. We've ended up…somewhere else."

"Like Narnia?"

"A bit—without the talking animals. This just looks a lot like our world, and we're going to find out how to get back. We think that's what the dreams are about. But we've got to go somewhere first. We've got to go to a place called Pendle Hill. Have you ever heard of it?"

Evan shook his head. "Is it in Wales? We go to Wales for our holidays."

"No—"

"Only you said hill, and there are hills in Wales."

"There are hills everywhere!" Emma put in, then caught Joey's eye and said, "Yes, I know, I know. Shutting up."

"It's not in Wales," Joey explained patiently. "It's in Lancashire. We think it'll take a day or two to walk there. We want you to come with us."

"I-I don't know," Evan stammered uncertainly. "Ruby doesn't walk fast. And she doesn't want to go anywhere in case..."

"In case your Mum comes back," Joey finished. "I know. But she left Formby, didn't she? She came this far with you. It's only a bit further. And then, if we don't find out how to get home, we'll take you back to Formby, I promise."

Evan thought for a moment. "I'll talk to her," he said. "Could you...?" He pointed to the entrance of the barn.

"Yes, of course." Joey took Emma by the arm and steered her away. "We'll be outside."

Once out in the courtyard, Emma lit a cigarette. "This is just great." She crumpled up the empty packet and put it in her pocket. "Just great. Now two bloody kids are running the show."

"I'm not leaving them." Joey felt like a stuck record. "If they won't come, I'll stay with them and you can go on without me."

"What?" Emma gasped, genuine shock on her face. "You can't do that! You've got to be there. It's all about you, Joey."

"No, it isn't. I'm nothing special."

"The way Remick made it sound, you're the frigging Messiah. You've got to be there."

"Then we'll have to hope Evan can talk Ruby round."

"If he doesn't," Emma said grimly, taking a drag on her cigarette, "I'll tie the little brat up and carry her."

"You'd make a terrible mother," Joey said without thinking.

"I learned from the best," was Emma's reply. But before she could elaborate further, Evan emerged from the barn with Ruby clinging to his arm, the stuffed badger in her other hand.

"We'll come," Evan said.

Chapter Sixteen

IN THE END, it was all a matter of compromise. Evan and Ruby agreed to come along but said they were tired and asked if they could stay the rest of the day at the farm and leave tomorrow. Emma, although impatient to get moving, reluctantly agreed, under the condition that they moved into the farmhouse. It would be safer if the Screamers came in the night. On being reminded of the 'noise with teeth', the children needed no further persuading. They all picked up their bags and crossed the courtyard to the farmhouse.

The front door was locked, and Emma was checking the windows to see if any could be forced open—Joey didn't like to enquire where she had acquired that particular skill—when suddenly, she jumped back with a cry of, "Jesus!" as a face appeared at the window. Evan looked back out at her, grinning. Ruby stood next to him, laughing like an idiot.

"Back door!" Evan shouted through the glass.

Emma muttered something under her breath, and Joey made a mental note to keep an eye on the kids. Neither he nor Emma had noticed they'd gone. They grabbed the bags and followed the kids around to the back of the building, where the door was wide open.

Inside, the farmhouse was big, cool and old-fashioned. The back door led straight into a large kitchen dominated by a heavy wooden table in the middle and a black cast iron stove at one end. The walls were lined with cupboards and shelves that held a vast array of china plates and cups, all of which looked old, possibly even antique.

Emma opened one or two of the cupboards and found them to be well stocked with food. "Who says farming doesn't pay?"

Joey, however, had found the answer. On a work surface near the door was a pile of leaflets and an A4-size diary. "Looks like they were running it as a bed-and-breakfast."

"That's pretty much what we're using it for," Emma replied.

Evan and Ruby burst into the kitchen, and again Joey was reminded he'd forgotten they were there.

"There's lots of rooms upstairs!" Evan said excitedly. "We've picked ours."

"That's great!" Joey found himself getting caught up in the boy's enthusiasm. "But they better hadn't be the best rooms, because they're ours."

"No, there's one with two beds in. That's all we need. There's a big one for you two."

With that, he disappeared again, presumably to join his sister in doing some more exploring.

"Hang on," Emma said, half surprised and half amused. "Do they think…?"

"We should have a look through these cupboards and find something to eat. I'm starving."

"Sounds like a plan. Do you cook?"

"A bit. You?"

"God, no. I can use a microwave. That's all I've ever needed."

"Looks like it's me, then. Let's see what we can find."

Joey rounded the kids up briefly, to find out what they liked to eat; they said they didn't mind and then rejected all his suggestions. After an inspection of the kitchen's packed freezer, he found two large pizzas. Those seemed to go down well with everyone.

Even though the kitchen had the cast iron range, there was also a conventional cooker next to it. Joey put the pizzas in, and he and Emma joined the kids upstairs to find their own rooms. Evan had been right. There were five bedrooms upstairs, and without any debate, he and Emma each picked one and dumped their bags. By the time the pizzas were ready, the sky was starting to darken.

They ate their meal around the table in the kitchen, even though the kids had wanted to eat in the lounge. While Emma silently attacked her pizza, Joey made conversation with Evan and Ruby. Evan was much more forthcoming, while Ruby only spoke very quietly, answering in one or two words at a time, and always looking to her brother for approval. Evan was happy to talk about his favourite football team—Liverpool—and his favourite subject at school—maths—but when asked about his family, he became less talkative. He said his mum worked in a coffee shop, but when Joey asked about his dad, all Evan was prepared to say was that he was 'gone'.

"What about your stepdad?" Joey asked. "What does he do?"

He knew he'd made a mistake when he saw a shadow cross the young boy's face. Ruby's reaction was even more dramatic. She positively shrank in her chair and gave her brother an imploring look. Joey realised the best thing to do was to leave the subject alone.

"So what do you guys want to do now?"

Evan and Ruby exchanged glances.

"I think we'd better just go to bed," Evan said. "We're a bit tired."

"That's okay. You go ahead."

The two kids got up silently and left the table. As they reached the kitchen door, Ruby turned and very quietly said, "Goodnight."

"Goodnight," Joey replied; Emma just waved vaguely.

It was only then that Joey became aware he had done all the talking during their meal while Emma had lapsed into silence. As soon as Evan and Ruby had gone, she, too, stood up and, without saying another word, snatched her jacket off the back of her chair and left the kitchen by the back door.

Joey sighed and cleared the table, putting the plates and cutlery in the sink and running some hot water onto them. He hunted in the cupboards and found a jar of instant coffee, let the kettle boil while he washed the dishes, then made himself a cup of coffee and took it into the lounge.

The owners of the farmhouse had gone to some effort to make the lounge comfortable. The furniture was not new, in keeping with the rest of the house, but when Joey sat down on the settee, he sank down into the cushions. As he waited for Emma to come back, he had a chance to reflect for the first time on the day's events. Heading off on a journey to Pendle for God knew what purpose was strange enough, but he had never expected to end the day in charge of two kids he'd only just met.

He remembered how his friend Sam was always complaining about his little sister, eight-year-old Morgan, who followed him around at home, hardly giving him a moment's peace. Yet whenever Joey was at Sam's house, he never heard any complaints. Sam was patient and kind with Morgan, listening to all she had to say and joining in with her nonsense and stories. It was all alien to only child Joey.

Now, he was in a position of responsibility to two children, and it made him feel uncomfortable and worried that he wasn't up to the task. Added to that was the unpleasant thought that Evan and Ruby clearly had issues with their stepdad. There was a whole other story there, and Joey wasn't sure he wanted to hear it.

He'd nearly finished his coffee by the time Emma returned. She came into the lounge and plonked herself down at the other end of the settee, huddled in her jacket. It was a good five minutes before she spoke.

"He's doing something to them, isn't he, the stepdad? Bastard."

"I think so. There's something."

"He hurts them. They're terrified, especially the girl."

Joey didn't reply.

"And we're trying to take them back to him. They're probably better off here."

"They can't stay on their own," Joey said. "What about their mum? She must miss them."

"If he's doing something and she's letting him stay, she's just as bad."

"We don't know the story. It's not for us to interfere. We just need to try and keep them safe and get them home."

"Yes, let's not interfere," Emma spat. "That's how bastards like him get away with it. Because people don't interfere."

"What about you?" Joey asked. "Don't you want to get home? Your parents must be worried about you. I know my mum and dad will be frantic."

"Good for you." Emma sneered. "My dad hasn't worried about me for years so I doubt he's going to start now. As for my mum... she probably hasn't noticed I'm gone."

"I'm sure that can't be true. The posters—"

"Look, Joey, you don't know anything about me. You haven't a clue."

"Then tell me," he said quietly.

Emma burst into tears, taking him completely by surprise. He let her cry without interruption. When the tears eventually subsided, she wiped her eyes on her sleeve and said, "Okay."

Chapter Seventeen

Emma Winrush had been quite a happy child. Even though, because of what came later, she found it hard to picture her early childhood, what she did remember was nothing spectacular, just a feeling of contentment.

An only child, she lived with her mother and father in Crosby, up the road from Waterloo. She didn't mind that she was an only child, particularly; she had friends in her street and at school, and spent a fair amount of time reading. She had a clear memory of her father reading to her when she was little, which gave her a love of books she carried for years.

Once she was old enough to choose what she read, she devoured Alice, and Narnia, and Harry Potter. She'd stopped reading when she was thirteen, when things started to go wrong. It was then that she discovered there was nothing to save her in the real world. Aslan the lion did not exist outside the pages of the book, and real people could not conjure up a Patronus to protect them. In the real world, bad things happened and there was nothing and no-one to help.

Two bad things happened at once, and they both happened to Emma's father. Barry Winrush had a corner shop, the kind that sells just about everything, from newspapers to groceries, to alcohol and lottery tickets. He worked long hours, up to see the papers in and often finishing long after the shop shut, if his evening staff let him down. The shop did reasonably well, despite the best efforts of the big supermarkets to price him out of business.

People were still loyal, shopping with Barry for the convenience. They paid a little more for their groceries, but the personal service made it worthwhile. Sometimes, after school and at weekends, Emma would help him out. Her dad taught her how to use the pricing gun, and Emma loved pricing things. The customers also loved seeing Barry's little daughter, then eleven or twelve, going around the shop with a serious look on her face, sticking price labels on tins and packets. Her mum, Sandra, also worked—as a mobile hairdresser—and there seemed always to be money for treats, meals out, books if Emma wanted them, a holiday once a year. But then the bad things happened, and everything stopped being fun.

First came the robbery and then the recession. One might have caused the other; there certainly seemed to be more crime around when the recession started to bite and people tried to find ways of saving pennies here and there. The papers were full of how it would mean everyone would have less money, offering helpful money-saving tips, the most important of which was *shop around*.

And people did. They would rather pay 15p for a tin of budget baked beans in a supermarket than pay for the branded beans in Emma's dad's shop. The customers who had once been so loyal deserted in droves, hurrying past with their budget supermarket carrier bags, unable to look her dad in the eye. Fewer people seemed to want their hair done, too, so her mum also had less work.

It was around that time Emma had to stop helping in the shop. There wasn't enough for one person to do, her dad said, let alone two. He was no fun to be around any more; he just stood behind the counter looking out onto his frequently empty shop, lines of worry etched into his face. Some days, he would sit in the small stockroom-cum-office, staring at piles of unpaid bills, his face like a crumpled piece of paper. Still, he would not desert the shop, and Emma heard her parents talking about it one night.

"We just have to ride it out," her father said. "Trade through it. It will get better. It has to."

She lay in bed wishing she could do something to help, but she was too young.

It was *probably* lucky she hadn't been in the shop the night of the robbery. She'd been at home with her mum.

Emma was in the living room doing her homework—those were the days when she still cared about school—when the phone rang. She heard the shocked gasp after her mum answered it… heard her put the phone down only to snatch it up again and call a taxi.

She came hurrying into the living room, pulling her coat on. "Em, you'll have to go next door to Margaret," she said, hunting in her handbag for purse, keys, mobile, anything she might need. Then she stopped, put her arms around her daughter and said the words which made Emma go light-headed and almost faint. "It's your dad. He's in hospital."

Emma wanted to go with her, but her mum refused and batted away all of Emma's questions. No, she didn't know what had happened. Yes, her dad was alive. No, she didn't know when she'd be back but would ring as soon as she could. When the ring-back from the taxi came, they both jumped, and her mum hustled Emma out of the door. Luckily, Margaret, their elderly neighbour, was in—but then, she usually was—and was happy to take Emma, who watched, worried and bewildered, as her mum ran to the taxi and sped away to the hospital.

Emma spent two anxious hours making small talk and drinking tea and not really watching the television with Margaret before the phone rang. She knew it was her mum because Margaret said 'yes', 'no' and 'I see' a lot. Her mum ended the call without wanting to speak to Emma, so it was from Margaret that Emma found out what had happened.

Her dad had been on his own in the shop. He'd had to let his evening assistant go a couple of weeks earlier because there simply wasn't the trade to justify the wages. Maybe the two men who came in knew that, or maybe they just took a chance.

They'd brought baseball bats with them, and when her dad tried to resist their attempts to rob his shop, one of them had hit him over the head. They had grabbed what they could, left him lying semi-conscious on the floor, and fled. A young couple who happened to be passing by had seen the men run out of the shop and called 999. Emma's dad, still conscious though barely, had been rushed by ambulance to A&E.

He'd spent two days in hospital before the doctors were happy there would be no lasting effects and sent him home. They were half right. He had a lump on his head and a nasty bruise, and there were no lasting physical effects. Mentally, though, the after-effects lasted a lot longer. He still spent long hours in the shop, but when he came home, he was quiet, tired and withdrawn. He and Emma's mum, who had always had what seemed to be a happy marriage, started arguing. Never in front of Emma; in other rooms so she didn't hear all of what it was about, but money came up over and over again. It wasn't a huge surprise, then, that her dad came home one day and announced he was selling the shop. He'd had a decent offer, he said, and it would be stupid to turn it down.

In a funny way, the months after the shop changed hands were the best months of that period. The family had some money for a change, and Emma's dad seemed happier now he didn't have to work such long hours. He even managed to get himself a job in one of the big supermarkets, the ones that had done all they could to put him out of business.

But it was this job in Asda that led to the third, and worst bad thing…

The last thing Emma had expected when she came home from school that Thursday in May, two weeks after she and her parents had been out for a nice Chinese meal to celebrate her fourteenth birthday…

Her dad was upstairs packing, and her mum was standing in the living room, tears pouring down her pale face. Her dad hardly spoke, except to say he was sorry but he had to go. Her mum, through her sobs, tried to explain that her dad was leaving them for 'some bitch he met at work'. And then, with a slam of the door, her dad was gone, leaving Emma on her own with her mum, and everything changed.

For Emma, it happened gradually, but the change in her mum was immediate. She lost interest in everything. She stopped taking bookings from the few clients she had left and spent her days in front of the television, pretending to watch whatever trash was on. Emma got her own tea when she came home—at least her mum made sure there was always food in—and her dad, for his part, made sure they were provided for.

After tea, Emma did her homework and watched nothing very much on the television with her mum until it was time for her to go to bed. Her mum always opened a bottle of wine in the evening and usually finished it before she went to bed. Emma never saw her drunk, and never questioned the wine.

This carried on for a year or so. Emma saw her dad once a month. He always met her away from wherever he was living now and always on his own. Whenever they met, he seemed to be forcing himself to be jolly, and Emma could tell he couldn't wait to get away. School became her refuge—at least her friends cared about her—but soon that changed too. Her friends started to go out after school, for burgers or to the cinema, and Emma never went with them.

Despite the fact she and her mum barely spoke to each other, Emma still didn't want to leave her on her own, so she declined all invitations and just went home. After a while, the invitations stopped, and Emma's friends drifted away, preferring to spend their time with each other. Emma began to feel increasingly alone, miserable and invisible. It was just after she turned fifteen, a birthday nobody really bothered about, that she cut herself for the first time.

The first time was an accident. She was making her tea and cutting some bread to go with it when the knife slipped and sliced into her hand. She watched with a horrible fascination as the blood soaked into the white bread, and then did what anyone would do; she went to her mum. And when Sandra saw her come into the living room with her hand raised and blood running down her arm, she was suddenly Mum again. She bathed the cut to see how deep it was and if it maybe needed stitches, then held a tea towel tight to the wound to staunch to the flow. When she was satisfied the cut wasn't as bad as it looked and a trip to the walk-in centre wouldn't be necessary, she found a box of plasters and dressed Emma's hand.

That evening, they sat and watched television together on the settee, her mum with her arm around her still-shocked daughter. For that evening, things were as they should be. But two days later, a letter arrived from her dad's solicitor, saying that he was finally filing for divorce, and her mum withdrew back into herself, back to the TV and the wine. The bottles seemed to stack up more and more quickly, and while Emma couldn't be sure, she thought she could detect alcohol on her mother's breath some evenings when she came home from school.

Her mum might have forgotten how good that one evening of closeness felt, but Emma hadn't. The next time she cut herself, it was deliberate. She was never sure where the idea came from, but she found herself in the kitchen holding a knife, pressing its tip to the back of her wrist. Keeping the tip of the blade pressed to her skin, she dragged the knife; it was barely a scratch, but when she took the knife away, there was a white mark, about an inch and a half long on her skin. She stared at the mark, feeling a strange thrill as tiny pin-pricks of blood bubbled up along the white line. Then she went into the living room and sat on the settee, her arm exposed on her lap waiting for her mum to notice, but she was watching what she pretended was one of her favourite shows with a bottle open by her side and didn't notice at all.

The following morning, the cut had dried to a gritty red line. Two days later, it had just about disappeared altogether. No-one ever noticed. Two weeks later, Emma did it again, and again, no-one noticed. It was then that the cutting changed from being something she did to draw attention to herself, to Emma's Secret. It was something she did to herself and for herself. She started wearing long-sleeved tops to hide the marks, which had become deeper than her first tentative scratch. She always took great care to use a clean knife and to bathe the wounds.

Apart from that, life carried on as normal, or the Winrush family's version of normal. Anyone who saw Emma, or at least, anyone who took the slightest notice, would have thought she was just a normal, rather quiet and sulky teenager. But when Emma looked at her arms and the scars criss-crossing them, she knew that she had a secret nobody knew.

She carried The Secret for over a year. She scraped through her GCSEs, although she was feeling less and less interested in school. She rarely spoke to anyone there but did her work despite a nagging feeling that there was little point. Why bother? There were no jobs around and her mum didn't care whether she did well or not. Her former friends were more interested in pairing up with boys, but none of the boys paid any attention to Emma.

She tried to have a conversation with her mum about whether to stay on for the sixth form or leave and get a job, but her mum just shrugged and said it was up to Emma. So Emma did her GCSEs, which coincided with her sixteenth birthday—again unmarked—and left school.

She drifted for six months, wandering the streets, pretending to look for a job but really not bothered either way. She dyed her hair purple, because she liked the colour, and started wearing heavy eyeliner because she liked the look. Nobody else noticed. She still cut herself from time to time, but her heart wasn't even in that any more. In fact, the memory of having just cut herself, lying in bed with her arm still stinging, and hearing her mum eventually come up to bed, was Emma's last memory of 'home'. The next morning she woke up and everyone had gone.

Chapter Eighteen

JOEY LISTENED WITHOUT interruption while Emma told her story. She stalled sometimes, and sometimes told the story in such a fragmented way it barely made sense. Still, he sat in silence while she talked, partly because he was afraid interrupting would make her clam up and never start again, but also because he simply did not know what to say. His own life was so far removed from Emma's he had nothing helpful to add.

"So there you go," Emma said when she reached the part when everyone in the world had vanished. "That's me. Still want to walk to Pendle with me?"

"I don't…" Joey began. "Poor you. You must have been lonely."

"Don't," Emma warned, some of the old steel coming back into her red-rimmed eyes. "Don't feel sorry for me. No, I don't do lonely. It taught me, Joey. It taught me I don't need anyone. I'm fine on my own. I've survived so far, haven't I?"

"Everyone needs someone," Joey replied, but it felt like a cliché even as he said it.

"Easy for you to say. I bet you had everything—two parents, friends, the lot."

"I had two parents who treated me like I'd drop down dead at any minute," Joey snapped. "They wouldn't let me do anything. And I'm fine. There's nothing wrong with me."

"At least they noticed you. They'll notice you've gone. My mum's probably glad I'm gone…if she's noticed at all."

The silence resumed, filling the minutes, until Emma broke it, repeating, "I'm fine on my own."

"But you're not on your own any more," Joey argued as gently as he could. "You've got me."

"That's sweet." Emma patted his leg and stood up. "But if we find a way back, we'll go our separate ways. You'll go back to your mum and dad, and I'll go back to whatever. See you in the morning. Then we'll get moving."

With that, she left and went upstairs.

Joey sat on his own looking at the door through which she had left. "It's just us till then," he said, only vaguely aware it was out loud. "We'll be okay."

He stared at the door for what felt like an age, but Emma didn't come back. Eventually, Joey also went to bed.

No Screamers came that night, or if they did, no-one heard. Joey, Emma and the two children slept soundly on.

Joey was wrong, though. By the time they all woke up, early the following morning, it wasn't just them any more, and it certainly wasn't okay.

Chapter Nineteen

RUBY HEARD THEM first. While the rest of the occupants of the farmhouse slept, she had woken early, fearful and restless, and hid beneath the covers in case the *horrible noise that screams and bites* came back. It was too warm, and she popped her head out and lay, listening apprehensively, in the dark. The noise was in the distance, breaking through the silence. It sounded like it was far away, but getting closer. She tried to wake Evan, but he just muttered sleepily that he couldn't hear anything, turned over and went back to sleep.

Ruby climbed out of bed, clutching Brian, her stuffed badger. Her mummy had given him that name and thought it very funny; Ruby had never been sure why. The name had stuck, and Brian went everywhere with Ruby. He came with her now as she crept out of the bedroom and onto the landing, where she stood listening. She wanted to find which room the Light Man was in but didn't want to disturb the Lady With The Cuts. Ruby knew all about disturbing the wrong people in the middle of the night. Geoff hated it and was always really cross when she had a bad dream and had to find Mummy.

She heard a male cough come from a room to her left, and nervously pushed the door open. "Hello?" Her voice came out as little more than a squeak.

The bedclothes rustled as they moved, and somewhere in the dark of the room, the Light Man muttered, "Emma?"

"It's me," Ruby said, louder now. "It's Ruby."

***

"Ruby? Is everything okay?" Joey hadn't realised how deeply he had been sleeping and wasn't sure why he'd made the assumption it was Emma coming into the room. When he heard it was Ruby, he shot out of bed, dressed only in T-shirt and boxer shorts.

"Has something happened?" he asked, switching the light on.

"They're coming!" Ruby said. "I heard them."

"What did you hear?" Joey went to her and crouched down. "Did you have a dream?"

"No," Ruby insisted. "I *heard* them. Can't you hear? They're coming!"

Joey stood up and listened intently. He heard only Ruby's breathing and the occasional creak from the farmhouse, but nothing else.

"I can't hear anything. You must've been dreaming. Come on. Let's get you back to bed."

But Ruby stood her ground and would not move.

"It's a car," she said. "Can't you hear it?"

"It can't be a car." Joey strained to hear despite himself. "There aren't any cars now. They're all stopped—" He broke off.

It can't be!

At first, he thought his mind was playing tricks, fooled by the suggestion Ruby had put into his head. But the more he listened, the more obvious it was. Somewhere in the distance, cutting through the still of the early morning, he could make out the sound of an engine, and for a moment, he was paralysed, unable quite to take in what he was hearing.

"Go and wake up Evan, Ruby," he ordered, steering the girl out of the room. He followed her onto the landing and banged hard on Emma's door, shouting, "Get up, Emma!" then raced back into his own room to get dressed. Once he'd pulled on trousers and sweatshirt, he ran downstairs, passing a barely awake Emma, who was just emerging from her room.

Downstairs, Joey checked the front and back doors were both firmly locked, then stood by the front door listening. The engine noise was getting louder, still a little way away, but definitely coming closer. Even though he knew little about cars, Joey could tell the engine wasn't in the best of health. Then the lights went out.

Joey whirled round and nearly jumped out of his skin when a voice right next to him said, "Range Rover, I reckon. Something like that."

"*God*, Emma!" Joey yelled, his heart pounding.

"If they're coming this way, lights probably aren't a good idea." There was unmistakable amusement in her voice.

"You heard, then?"

"Yes. I don't know how the kid heard before us, though. Hopefully, they'll pass by."

They listened once more.

"It's stopped," Joey said. "I think they've gone. You can't see this place from the road, anyway."

"Still, leave the lights off for now. You staying up?"

"Not much point going back to bed."

"Well stick the kettle on, then. No-one can see that from outside."

"Whoever it was," Joey said, feeling his way into the kitchen, "I'm pretty sure they've gone."

The kids went back to bed, and Joey and Emma sat in the living room as the dark turned slowly into a murky grey. They kept themselves awake with coffee, sometimes talking about nothing very much and sometimes just listening. They didn't hear the engine again, because there was no engine to hear.

They came on foot, and they came quietly, and when Joey cautiously peeked out from behind the kitchen blinds while he was boiling the kettle for yet another coffee, they were there. Three of them, standing patiently in the courtyard, waiting for any sign of life from the farmhouse.

Chapter Twenty

THERE WERE TWO men and a woman. One of the men and the woman looked like they were supporting the other man, who seemed to have difficulty standing. He looked to be in his fifties, or possibly younger, but his hair was greying at the temples, which made him look older. He wore a dark-coloured suit and a shirt with no tie. There was dust on the knees of his suit trousers, and one sleeve of his jacket was torn. The man and woman supporting him were definitely younger, dressed in leather jackets, jeans and band T-Shirts. They looked for all the world like they had left their motorbikes somewhere.

It wasn't the leather jackets, however, that made Joey drop the blind like it was hot and rush back into the living room to get Emma. Nor was it the fact that the three of them were just standing there, staring at the farmhouse. No, what really bothered him was the rifle slung over the biker man's shoulder.

"Emma," he hissed as he hurried into the living room. "We've got company."

Emma, who had been drowsing on the settee, sat bolt upright. "Where?"

Joey nodded his head toward the outside. "Three of them. One looks a bit out of it, but the other two aren't. One's got a gun."

"Are the doors locked?"

"Yes. I checked before."

Emma nodded her approval. "Then let's just lie low, keep quiet and wait them out."

"That won't work," Joey argued. "I think they're waiting for us. They know we're here, Emma."

With Joey following behind, Emma crept into the kitchen and, standing to one side, lifted the blind a fraction. She glanced out, then put the blind back.

"You're right," she said.

"You think so?"

"I know so. The woman just waved at me."

"Oh, great." Joey scowled. "Now what? Can we get out the back?"

"With the kids? I don't think so. Anyway, we're only assuming it's just them. They might have mates round the back."

"So what do we do?"

Emma thought for a second, then pulled a carving knife from the knife block on the work surface and, after weighing it in her hand, tucked it into her belt at the small of her back.

"Let's go and talk to them."

"Are you out of your mind?" Joey was aghast.

"Well, they're not going anywhere. Let's go and see what they want."

Before Joey could stop her, she had turned the key in the door and stepped outside. Joey grabbed a knife for himself, realising on his way to the door that he'd picked a small fruit knife. He tossed it onto the worktop and followed Emma outside.

She stood facing the strangers. No-one was saying anything, but that changed when Joey arrived. As soon as they saw him, the face of the man in the leather jacket broke into a broad grin.

"Here he is!" he said in an accent which was not quite Liverpool. "We've had a bit of a trip to come and find you, mate."

"Who are you?" Joey asked. "What do you want?"

"I'm Dave." The man gestured to the woman. "This is Anna."

"All right?" she said, smiling too.

"Don't know what our friend's name is," Dave said, tilting his head towards the man they were propping up. "He doesn't talk much."

"What do you want?" Emma repeated Joey's question. Joey saw her reach behind her back and touch the knife's handle.

"Can we go inside to talk?" Dave asked. "He's getting a bit heavy, and I don't want to drop him."

"We can talk here," Emma said. Dave ignored her and continued watching Joey, who held his ground.

"Like she said. We can talk here."

Dave's expression turned angry. "Now wait a minute, we've come—"

"Dave," Anna interrupted. "The gun. I told you not to bring it."

"What?" Dave frowned but then grinned again. "This? Oh, hell, sorry. I found it. Brought it along because you can't be too safe. I don't know if it's loaded, even. Look, can we at least put our friend here down? He's in a bad way."

Joey looked to see what Emma thought. She shrugged and turned away. *Your call.*

"Bring him inside," Joey said, "but leave the gun out here."

In the end, Joey had to take over from Dave in supporting the other man, while Dave unslung the rifle from his shoulder and rested it against the farmhouse wall. Between them, Joey and Anna steered the other man inside and onto the settee in the living room. His head slumped onto his chest, and for a moment, Joey thought he was dead, until the man coughed, then started breathing heavily and noisily, apparently asleep. Now he could see more closely, Joey realised the man wasn't as old as he'd first thought, forties at the most. He was slim, almost thin, and had the sharpest cheekbones Joey had ever seen.

"Right, then," Dave said cheerily, making himself comfortable in one of the armchairs. "Any chance of a cuppa?"

Chapter Twenty-One

EMMA TOLD JOEY to get the kettle on. She needed to go to the loo—all the coffee they'd drunk, she said—but Joey knew there was something else behind it. He hadn't expected her to be so hospitable, and as he put the kettle on, he realised what it was. The kids. *Of course.* He'd forgotten about Evan and Ruby. He heard the toilet flush, and Emma came into the kitchen, closing the door behind her.

"I've told them to stay up there," she whispered. "At least till we find out what this lot want."

"I don't like this," Joey said. "I don't trust them."

"Well, you let them in," Emma pointed out but reassured him with a half-smile.

"We've only got his word the gun isn't loaded. And they seem to know who I am. Let's at least find out why."

Without asking anyone what they wanted, Joey made coffees all round, and he and Emma took the drinks through to the living room. The woman, Anna, was sitting with her feet tucked under her on the end of the settee not occupied by their sleeping companion.

She took a cup of coffee from Emma with a grateful smile. "Thanks. I need this."

There followed an uneasy silence while they sipped their coffee. In the end, it was Anna who spoke first.

"We're not here to cause any trouble. I understand why you don't trust us, but this is all a bit weird for us, too."

"What are you doing here?" Emma asked. She was perched on the edge of an upright chair near the door, unable to sit back with the knife still tucked into her belt. "How come you're looking for Joey?"

"He's called Joey?" Anna asked. "At least we know that, now. And you are?"

"Emma."

"Great!" Dave exclaimed, with another grin. "Now we all know each other. Well, apart from sleeping beauty over there."

"Why are you looking for Joey?" Emma asked again.

"It's a bit of a long story," Dave said.

"Then you'd better get on with it."

It was Anna who told the story, with Dave sometimes chipping in. They had come from Warrington, which was as deserted as everywhere else. They'd set off some time ago, but they weren't sure how long, exactly. Anna, a nurse before all of this, had found herself in what seemed like an empty town. After a night out with friends and a heavy drinking session, she'd fallen asleep in a bus shelter, waiting for the last bus home, and had awoken several hours later with the worst hangover she'd had in years. According to her watch, it was four in the morning, and she'd started to walk home, hoping to find an all-night café on the way and not altogether surprised that there was nobody around.

She'd made it to her flat about an hour later and crashed out on the settee. By the time she woke up again, it was early afternoon, and there was still nobody around. It was then that she started to panic. She thought about who she could call—family, friends, even the police—but she couldn't get a signal on her phone. By early evening, it had started to sink in that she was on her own. That night, huddled in her bed, she'd heard the terrible screaming noise for the first time and convinced herself she'd gone mad.

She spent several days wandering around the town, looking for someone, anyone, and had eventually found Dave slumped in the corner of a bar. When he sobered up, he was able to tell her that he'd had a similar experience, but instead of trying to find anyone else, he'd ended up in the bar, doing his best to drink it dry. Anna joined him, and between them, they had another go.

In one of their more sober moments, they had become lovers and had stayed together ever since. They spent their time in the bar, or in the flat above it, and it didn't occur to them that there was anyone else left in the world.

"But then Dave started having the dreams—the same dreams I was having," Anna said.

"Dreams?" Joey asked.

"There's a lot of it about," Emma muttered drily.

"We didn't take much notice at first," Anna carried on. "Like, the screaming noise whirling round the pub every night was just something else to blot out with alcohol. But the dreams became too persistent to ignore. So, we decided to leave the pub in search of the young man we kept dreaming about, found a four-by-four with the keys in, and off we went."

"But the roads are all blocked," said Joey. "How did you get through?"

"Stayed on the main roads," Dave explained. "Just shoved everything out of the way. I think that's why the car packed in. It was falling to bits."

"What about him?" Emma pointed to the still sleeping figure on the settee.

"Found him in the middle of the road just outside Prescot," Dave said. "I wanted to leave him there, but Anna said no."

"He was the first person we'd seen," Anna reasoned. "We had to help him."

"And here we are," Dave finished.

"I need a fag," Emma announced, standing up. "Coming, Joey?"

She strode out into the courtyard and pulled a new packet of cigarettes out of her coat pocket. She tore off the cellophane and foil and lit one, inhaling deeply.

"What did you think?" she asked.

"I don't know."

"I do. I think it's the biggest load of bullshit I've heard in my life! The dreams Remick and the kids had were of you at Pendle, not here. How did they find us? There's something they're not telling us."

"Do you think they've been following us?"

"Not in the car. We'd have seen or heard them. And what's the deal with the guy they said they found in the road? That doesn't ring true, either. I don't like this, Joey. It stinks. We need to get the kids and get out of here."

"Thought you might say that," a voice said from behind them.

Joey turned to find Dave standing in the farmhouse doorway. He had a weeping Ruby in front of him. One arm was tight around her chest. In his other hand was a knife, the blade pressed against the girl's throat.

"Now get back inside," he snarled. "We've got lots to talk about."

Chapter Twenty-Two

LET THE GIRL go," Emma demanded, and Joey's heart sank. He should have known it wouldn't be so easy. Things could go very bad very quickly, especially if Emma chose this moment to pull her knife out.

"Come inside and I'll let her go," Dave said.

Joey intervened. "We're coming in. Just let her go. She's terrified." He stepped between Emma and Dave, holding up his empty hands. "You've got a knife. We're not going to try anything. Just let the kid go."

But Dave didn't relent. He held the struggling Ruby tighter and jerked his head towards the door of the farmhouse. He wanted Joey and Emma to go in first, and there was a real danger he'd see the knife Emma was concealing if he got behind her. Joey quickly decided to take a chance. Grabbing Emma by the arm, and ignoring her protests, he pushed her in front of him, blocking Dave's view with his body as he followed her into the farmhouse, with Dave and his young captive bringing up the rear.

Two sights greeted Joey as he entered the living room. One was that Anna had Evan pinned down on the settee. The other, rather more surprising sight was that the man in the suit, who had seemed so completely out of it when they had gone outside, was not only awake, but standing in the middle of the living room and appeared to be in charge.

"You're back," he said. "Good. Dave, the girl's got a knife in the back of her belt. Didn't you notice?"

Dave released Ruby, and she ran to Joey, who crouched to put his arms around her while she sobbed into his chest.

Dave advanced on Emma who pulled the knife out of her belt and held it out in front of her. "Do you want to take it from me?" she growled.

"Oh, put it down, Emma," the man in the suit said. "You'll cut yourself. Not that it would be anything new, would it?" He smiled. "Look, there's no need for any of this. We've got off to a bad start here. Let's all just calm down before someone gets hurt."

Emma hesitated, looking from Dave to the suited man, trying to assess who was the bigger threat. Dave took the opportunity to seize Emma's wrist, twisting it and making her drop the knife. Joey wanted to go to Emma's aid, but Ruby was clinging to him so tightly he couldn't move. It was, however, Suit Man who dealt with the situation.

"Dave!" he snapped. "I said no-one is to be hurt. Now, let her go, and step away."

Dave glared at the man in the suit but did as he was told.

"Right. Good. I think it's time for some introductions."

"You know who we are," Joey said. "How?"

"All in good time. But I should introduce myself. My name is Mr. Saunders. I apologise for the—shall we say—act I put together to gain access to this house. It was necessary because I suspect that you, and I mean Miss Winrush in particular, might have been reluctant to let us in otherwise."

"You got *that* right," Emma responded.

Saunders looked at her and raised a finger to his lips. "You've got spirit, I'll grant you that," he said pleasantly. "But it won't get you very far. What you need is information, and I can supply that. I can tell you all you need to know about where you are and how you can get home."

Over the top of Ruby's head, Joey stared at him. Emma was doing the same.

"Go on," Joey said.

"First, I need you to promise me something. I need you to promise that you will do exactly as I say, and I mean *exactly*."

"Why should we believe anything you say?" Emma demanded.

"I appreciate my actions so far might make you rather mistrustful, but desperate times call for desperate measures. It is, of course, entirely up to you whether you believe me or not. If you don't, that's fine. We'll just walk away now and not trouble you further. But if we do, you will stay here and never see your homes again."

"We don't need you," Emma said. "We know where we're going."

"Yes, of course." Joey really didn't like Saunders' smile. "Pendle Hill. Fine. Carry on to Pendle. But I will tell you one thing. These dreams that are taking you there do not tell the whole story. You will need to go there, yes, but not yet. Anyway, I can see you have made your minds up. Come on, Dave, Anna. We're wasting our time."

With that, he started walking towards the door.

"Wait," Joey said. "What do you mean, not yet? Is there somewhere else we need to go first?"

Saunders laughed. "You don't get me like that, Joey. Promise, and I'll tell you. Don't promise and you'll always wonder."

He paused in the doorway and looked from Joey to Emma and back again.

"What's it to be? Do you want to stay here childminding these two?" He gestured toward Evan, who was cowering where Anna had left him on the settee. "Or do you want to go home? Bear in mind these two poor little ones want to see their mummy again. You're not just responsible for yourselves now."

Before Emma could argue, Joey cut in. "All right. Tell us what you know."

Saunders' grin was humourless. "Promise first."

"We promise," Joey said without consulting Emma.

"Excellent! Now, you'd better sit down. You're going to have a great deal to take in."

Chapter Twenty-Three

J OEY HOPED EMMA might sit with him out of solidarity, but she sulked in the armchair while Evan and Ruby sat either side of him. Saunders sat in the other armchair. Where Dave and Anna had got to, Joey was not sure.

"The first thing is that you are not on Earth any more, or not on the version of it you know," Saunders began. "But then, you've already worked that out. I'll tell you what I believe this place is in a minute. I think I may have been the first person here. I've been here a long time."

Without waiting for any further discussion, Saunders proceeded to tell his story.

He had, he said, been one of those people who were usually called 'Something in the City' and had done well out of the boom times. He had it all: wealth, the best car, the finest house and a beautiful wife and child. He was even able to put enough aside to see him and his family through the leaner times that followed. But in the end, it was his wealth that ruined his life. If he had not been able to buy such an expensive car, his wife might not have died. She was driving it the day two masked men appeared out of nowhere at the traffic lights and tried to open the car doors to steal it.

Saunders' wife had panicked, hit the accelerator without looking and hurtled across the junction into the path of a lorry carrying a skip loaded with rubble from a nearby building site. It wasn't just his wife who died when the car was demolished; his eight-year-old daughter was in the car too. Saunders paused to wipe his eyes, though Joey was convinced there was nothing there to wipe.

Then followed what Saunders called his 'Lost Time', when he tried to dull the pain of his loss by drinking and taking whatever drugs he could get. With his money, he could get plenty. He had no idea what he did or where he went during that time. All he knew was he ended up on a beach in what he later discovered was Norfolk. When he gathered his wits enough to come off the beach and find the nearest town—Cromer—he found it was empty of people.

For a while, he'd thought he was going mad, but after a day or two, he realised he wasn't losing his mind at all. He felt strangely fit, more healthy than he had since his wife's and daughter's deaths. He had no desire for alcohol or drugs and started to understand it was not just he who had changed; it was the world. There really were no people in Cromer. Cars were paused in the middle of the road, as if all of a sudden, all their occupants had departed, leaving their vehicles where they were. Saunders started to walk, quickly discovering that whatever had happened had not just happened to Cromer. It was everywhere.

The lack of people was not the only thing he noticed. He consulted newspapers to find that there were significant differences between the world he had left and the world in which he had found himself.

"Different president," Joey interrupted.

"Not just in the States. Germany, Poland, Sweden…probably more, but I stopped looking."

Like Joey, Saunders had also observed the slight differences in some brand names and had come to the conclusion fairly rapidly that the population of the world, or at least, those parts of it he had seen, had not gone anyway; he had. As soon as he understood that, he began to explore this strange new world, looking at it through new eyes.

"You've noticed the thing about the food in the shops, I take it?" he asked.

"It doesn't go off," Joey said.

"More than that. It doesn't run out. I worked that out quite early on. I have—how can I put it?—*individual* tastes. There are things I like to eat, and things that I really do not like. I have what I suppose you'd call an obsessive personality. When I stayed for a while in a place on the outskirts of Norwich, I found food I liked in a small shop. I worried about what I would do when the stocks ran out. I'd have to move on, I thought.

"But the stocks didn't run out. It was a positive cornucopia. You know about the cornucopia, I take it?" On seeing the blank looks he received, he explained, "The cornucopia, or Horn of Plenty, has its origins in myth, though the myths tend to disagree about where exactly it came from. Whatever the case, when filled with food or drink, it never ran out.

"That was how it was with my shop, and it seems to be the case with every shop, the store cupboards in every house I've stayed in… And *that* is the key to understanding precisely what is going on here. This is the bit where you'll be glad you're sitting down."

Saunders paused—for dramatic effect, Joey thought. He felt a small kick in the side of his leg and realised that, at some point during Saunders' tale, both Evan and Ruby had fallen asleep. The kick was Ruby shifting in her sleep.

"Probably best," Saunders said, nodding at the children. "They won't understand any of this. Even I don't know how this world came to be. Nor can I explain the flaws in it—the differences in people's names, brand names… I do, however, believe I know *what* it is. I believe it is a single piece of time, and it repeats over and over again, maybe endlessly."

"Bullshit," Emma interrupted, speaking for the first time since they had sat down. "You're making this up."

"Fine," Saunders replied angrily. "Have it your way. I'm making it up. So you explain it, then. You explain everything and I'll listen to you. And while you're at it, tell me why I would make up something as ridiculous as that." He stared at Emma, who could not hold his gaze and looked away. "You can't, can you?" Saunders' tone seemed to soften. "Look, I know it's a lot to take in. But I have been here a lot longer than you. I have had a great deal more time to think, and I cannot come up with a better explanation. I can only keep coming back to that one. I also believe there is a way to break out of it. But I'm getting ahead of myself. There are things you need to understand, first.

"The first is that I was alone here for several months before I encountered anyone else. During that time, I wandered from town to town, trying to find out what had happened to me and just living. Those things you call Screamers? They are quite a recent thing. I never heard or saw them during those first few months. It was only when I became aware I was not alone that they began to appear." Saunders paused again. Then he coughed once and grimaced. "I'm sorry. All this talking is making my mouth dry. Emma, do you think you could get me a glass of water or something?"

Emma did not reply but rolled her eyes and flounced out to the kitchen. As soon as she had gone, Saunders leaned forward urgently and spoke to Joey in a quiet voice, glancing towards the door as he did so. "I don't think she believes me."

"I'm not sure I do," Joey replied.

"But you are more open-minded than Emma. It's vital you do everything you can to convince her."

He stopped speaking then, and Emma returned with a cold bottle of water. Saunders thanked her, but kept eye contact with Joey who, for his part, could not look at Emma. Even though he had agreed to nothing, he still felt complicit and treacherous.

Saunders opened the bottle of water, took a long swig, and then continued with his story.

Chapter Twenty-Four

L IKE JOEY, THE first person Saunders encountered was a tramp. At the time, he was staying in a small town on the coast, and had been wandering around, as was his habit. He was on his way back to the house he was using when he heard the unmistakable sound of a human voice. He peered around a corner and saw the figure of a man dressed in ragged clothes shuffling along and talking to himself. Saunders was so surprised to see another human being, he nearly rushed over to speak to him. But he held back as he realised the conversation this man was having with himself was nonsense.

"I don't know what state he was in before he arrived," Saunders said, "but his mind was completely gone."

Saunders returned to his house quickly, not wanting to be noticed. It was starting to get dark by then, and as night fell, he heard his first Screamer.

"I don't need to tell you what it's like to hear one for the first time. Terrifying. Terrifying."

He cowered inside his house, and under the hideous noise of the Screamer, he heard human, male screams too. He never saw the tramp again.

Thinking the Screamer only inhabited that town, Saunders moved on the next day. But the night's events had taught him two lessons. One was that he needed to be careful because there were still things, dangerous things, he had not come across. The other was that there might be other people here—people with more sanity than the unfortunate tramp—and he resolved to find them.

"And that is what I have been doing," Saunders said, taking another swig of water. "I have travelled the length and breadth of the country trying to find more people."

"There are plenty of places with no people at all. Sometimes I could go for days, even weeks, without seeing a soul. But from time to time, I would meet them, usually singly, sometimes more than one. We'd talk, I'd listen to their stories, pick up what information I could, then move on. Those stories are remarkably similar—all people who've found themselves here quite recently, though it varies from days to weeks. They're all bewildered and scared to one extent or another. And they all have dreams. As I listened, I saw a pattern. A teenage boy and girl appeared in them all. A hill, a field… And no," Saunders said in answer to an unasked question, "I don't dream myself. Never have.

"But there was one person I met who had a different dream. Somewhere near Shrewsbury, I encountered an elderly Asian lady who was living in a tent by the side of the road. She made me tea and explained she lived in the tent because she didn't want to invade someone else's house, even if there was nobody there.

"She seemed quite relaxed with the situation and told me about the dreams she had, in which her late husband appeared and spoke to her. He told her about a boy. A boy who would find a key himself, all alone, then take it to what she called 'The Witch Hill' and use it to unlock the world."

"Hang on," Joey broke in. "Alone?"

"That's what she said. Which is why it was imperative I found you. Everyone else who talked about you said you were travelling with a girl. Some people mentioned the children. But this woman was the only one who said you did something on your own first."

"But what?"

"All in good time," Saunders replied. "Not long after I left the Asian woman and headed north, I met up with Dave and Anna in Warrington, who were, as they had said, living a squalid, drink-fuelled existence in a pub. Again, we exchanged stories, and they insisted on accompanying me. Other people had suggested it before and I always resisted, but this time I agreed.

"Whether it was the after-effects of all the alcohol they'd consumed or some other reason, these two—Anna in particular—had very vivid dreams. In one, she saw the two of you walk past a road sign and was able to recall it pointed to Ormskirk and Preston, which is how I found out where you were. And that is pretty much my story."

"No," Emma said. "Just no. Thanks for telling us the story, but it would have been a better idea to come up with one that makes sense."

"I can assure you that everything happened just as I said," Saunders replied, sounding wounded. "Everything."

"Then how come all these people knew about us, what, weeks, months ago? Those two out there…they knew we were heading this way, when? A few days ago? We only left yesterday. Joey has been here less than a week. None of it makes sense."

"I can only tell you what I heard," Saunders said. "I didn't say I could explain it."

"And all that stuff about this world being one 'piece of time' that repeats itself? That sounded great, really convincing. But it's bollocks. You didn't think it through."

"I can assure you—"

"When do the Screamers come out?"

"I don't—"

"*When*, Saunders?"

"At night, but—"

"Well, if this world is one bit of time or whatever, where the hell does the night come from?"

"A day, then," Saunders said. "Maybe the piece of time is a day. I don't really know."

"You don't know because it isn't true. You're a liar, Saunders. Come on, Joey, wake the kids up. We need to get going. You can stay here or get lost, *Mr. Saunders*, but we're going to Pendle."

"I'm afraid that won't be possible." Saunders stood up. "You made a promise."

"And you lied to us." Joey stood up too. "Emma's right."

"A promise is a promise," Saunders said to them, then to someone else, "You can come in now."

Joey looked around and saw Dave and Anna standing in the living room doorway. Dave had retrieved the rifle from outside, and Anna was holding what looked like a handgun.

"You promised to do what I ask," Saunders said. "I don't want to hurt anyone, but I don't think you understand how important this is. Joey will leave on his own—I'll tell him where he needs to go. Emma, you and the children will come with us to Pendle, where we will wait for Joey."

"I don't think so," Emma said defiantly. "I'm going with him. He's useless on his own."

"Thanks!" Joey said with a touch of sarcasm, but he felt a huge amount of gratitude to Emma. She, in the meantime, had turned her attention to Dave and Anna.

"Try shooting us. Where will it get you? You need us, or so you say."

"No-one's going to shoot you," Saunders said peaceably. "But if you don't agree, and agree right now, I'll get Dave to shoot one of the children."

Chapter Twenty-Five

THERE WAS A long, tense silence, broken only by sobs and sniffles from not just Ruby but also her brother. The sight of a gun being pointed at them was too much even for Evan's bravery.

"I won't ask again," Saunders said.

Emma moved first, but surprised everyone by moving to stand between Dave and the children. She glared at him hatefully. "Thought you said the gun wasn't loaded."

"That was just to keep you happy. Of course it's loaded. Do you think I'm stupid?"

"I don't know." Emma gave him a sweet smile. "Let me think."

"Oh, shoot her," Saunders said dismissively. "The boy's the important one."

"Yeah?" Emma challenged. "I'm in the dreams too, knobhead, or had you forgotten that?"

There was a *click* as Dave took the safety catch off the rifle. He raised it to his shoulder, the barrel pointing at the centre of Emma's forehead.

"Well, come on!" she shouted. "I've got nothing to go back for, anyway!"

"No!" Joey stepped forward, standing side by side with Emma. "No-one's shooting anybody. What do I have to do?"

"Joey, don't be stupid…" Emma began, but Joey ignored her.

"I've had enough. I think Emma's right, Mr. Saunders or whatever your name is. I don't think you're telling us the whole truth. But if I need to go somewhere or do something so this whole thing can end and we can go home, then I'll do it. So where do I have to go? And what do I have to do?"

"That's more like it." Saunders motioned to Dave to lower the gun. "I'm glad one of you has sense. Now, come on. Let's all sit down like civilised people."

Still keeping one eye on Dave, Joey sat on the settee between Ruby and Evan. Ruby immediately cuddled into his side, burying her head in his chest. Evan looked at him with round wide eyes.

"He's got a gun," he uttered as if it were only just sinking in.

"Shh, Evan," Joey comforted. "He's not going to use it. He's only pretending."

"She's got one too!"

"I know. I know, Evan. It's okay. No-one's going to hurt you. I promise."

"Emma," Saunders said, a low threat in his voice. "Sit down."

Emma shrugged and sat in an armchair. Saunders sat in the other; Dave and Anna waited, alert and watchful, by the door.

"Good." Saunders smiled like they'd all just sat down for a pleasant cup of tea. "There's a reason I had to find you and stop you getting any further. The simple fact is you left too soon. But first, let me answer your questions, or as well as I can. You asked how there can be night if this world is, as I believe it to be, one repeated period of time. Truthfully, I don't know. I have theories that make sense to me, but there are still things I don't know. I don't know what the things you call Screamers are, where they come from or what they want."

"What about the dreams?" Joey asked. "How did people dream about me before I came here?"

"I don't know that either. Time here is a funny thing. Have you noticed that? Some days seem shorter than they should be. Some are about right. It's a bit difficult to tell what time of year it is. I don't think this world is very stable. I don't know why so many of the people I've met have had dreams about you. But because so many people *have* had these dreams, it would be foolish to ignore them. Especially the old Asian woman whose dream was different."

"What did she say?" Joey asked. "What did she say I have to do?"

"It wasn't very clear. She told me you were at home, and that the Iron Men had the key, but then she said it was somewhere else. She didn't say where."

"Somewhere else? What does that mean? It could be anywhere. What kind of key?"

"I wish I could tell you. I think you're just going to have to go home and look. Hopefully, this key will make sense when you see it."

"Another place," Emma said.

Saunders looked at her.

"What did you say?"

"Another place," Emma repeated. "She didn't say 'somewhere else', she said 'Another Place'. It's the Iron Men, Joey."

"You know what she meant by Iron Men?" Saunders asked.

"It's a thing on Crosby beach, by where we live," Joey explained. "Some guy made, like, a hundred metal sculptures of himself and planted them on Crosby beach. It's an art thing. It's called 'Another Place' but everyone calls them the Iron Men."

"That's it!" Saunders said triumphantly. "That's where you have to go. That's where you'll find the key, whatever it might be."

"But there's a hundred of them," Joey protested. "How do I know which one?"

"You don't," Saunders told him. "You'll just have to look. And I suggest you start moving now."

Chapter Twenty-Six

JOEY DIDN'T TAKE long to pack. He'd only taken a change of shirt and socks so stuffed the previous day's clothes back in the bag and came downstairs.

"Right." He entered the living room, his bag slung over his shoulder. "I'll be off, then."

"No time like the present," Saunders said, his face showing no emotion.

Joey looked over at Evan and Ruby, who were fearfully gazing up at him from the settee. He dropped his bag and went over, putting an arm around each of them. Ruby immediately buried her face in his shoulder.

"Don't want you to go," she whispered, her tiny voice muffled by Joey's jacket.

"Listen," Joey lifted her face so she could see him, "there's nothing to worry about. I'll be following really soon, but there's somewhere I've got to go first."

"We'll go with you," Evan offered.

"I'm sorry, I've got to go on my own, but I'll catch you up in a couple of days."

"That's right," Saunders interrupted. "And if Joey goes now, he'll be back even quicker."

Joey gave the two children a hug then stood up. He grabbed his bag and headed for the door.

"I'll see you off," Emma said.

"Don't keep him long," Saunders warned. "He has things to do."

Emma followed Joey out to the courtyard where they stood for a moment, each waiting for the other to speak.

"I'd best make a move," Joey said. "Sooner I go, the sooner I'll catch you up." He took a step away, and paused. "I don't like leaving you with Saunders."

"I can look after myself," Emma replied.

"As long as you do. I don't believe a word he says."

Joey was surprised, but pleased, when Emma threw her arms around him and hugged him tightly.

"Look after yourself, Joey Cale," she murmured.

"You too, Emma Winrush."

The kiss she planted on his cheek was so quick he wondered afterwards if it had happened at all. As soon as she had done it, she pushed him away.

"Now go on, get lost."

Joey nodded and headed for the gate, where he paused again and waved, then disappeared behind a hedge.

**

Emma stared after him for what felt like an age, wondering if that was the last time they'd see each other. Shaking herself out of her trance, she withdrew the battered packet of cigarettes from her pocket, lit one and took a long drag, soon realising she didn't want it after all. She dropped it and ground it out with her foot, then went back into the farmhouse.

Judging by the noises coming from the kitchen, Dave and Anna were shoving everything they could find into bags to take with them. Saunders was in the living room, looking out of the window with his back to her.

"Said goodbye to your boyfriend?" he asked.

"He's not..." Emma began but for once found herself not wanting to finish the sentence.

"Let's hope he is successful," Saunders said. "For all our sakes. I suppose we will know soon enough. In the meantime, Miss Winrush, I have other plans for you."

He turned then, and Emma saw his eyes, or rather, she saw the red, fiery pits where his eyes had been. It was all she could do not to scream and scream.

PART TWO

Chapter One

JOEY WALKED, TRYING not to think about why he was walking or what he was leaving behind. Even a friendly kiss on the cheek from Emma was a bit too much to contemplate right now. He had to concentrate on getting to where he had to go, doing what he had to do and catching up with Emma and the kids as soon as possible.

But pushing her out of his mind proved difficult. He had only known her a matter of days, and for a large part of that time, she had been narky and sarcastic. In truth, Joey had never known anyone like her. Since primary school, he'd not had much to do with girls. His school was a boys' school, and even on the occasions when his school came together with the neighbouring girls' school, its students seemed a different breed.

The cooler kids spent their time vying for the girls' attention, and quite a few of the lads in his year had girlfriends. But people like Joey and Sam were invisible to the girls and kept themselves that way, just getting on with what they were doing. There were girls of Joey's age in his neighbourhood, some he had known all his life, but these days, they hung out with people from their own schools and, although Joey was on a nodding-acquaintance basis with some of them, he didn't really mix with them.

Emma was different. She talked to Joey like he was if not exactly an equal, certainly something near. And now, after becoming something like friends, they were separated. Joey was on his own again, heading back to Waterloo to root around on the beach for God knew what.

It was hard for him to reconcile the person he was with the person he was now expected to be. Joey Cale, back in the world he knew, was a reasonably good student, waiting to get what he thought would be quite good A' Level results, but otherwise nothing remarkable. Other kids were better at sports, better academically, better fighters, more popular. Joey was just 'okay' at most things. Yet here he was, expected to find the answer to get them home, and then do what? He wasn't sure, but people were dreaming about it—about *him*—and with every step he took, the weight of responsibility grew heavier and heavier, until he had to stop at the side of the road to think about it.

As he sat, staring at the tableau of cars, frozen like a movie on which someone had pressed pause, he wanted to walk away from it all, and keep walking until someone took the responsibility from him. He wanted it all to go away.

Opening his bag to get a bottle of water out of it, he noticed something that should not be there. Somehow Ruby's stuffed badger had found its way into Joey's backpack. Maybe he'd picked it up accidentally, or maybe she'd slipped it in there while he wasn't looking. Either way, there it was, and Joey knew there and then that he had to complete his mission and catch up with the others so he could return the badger to Ruby. He drank some of the water and repacked his bag with the badger's head poking out as if to keep watch, slung the bag on his shoulder and got up and got moving.

Joey kept to the main road. It was the only route he knew back to Waterloo—the route his father had driven each time they came this way. Although it occurred to him there had to be a quicker, more direct way, he didn't want to risk wasting time with wrong turns. He would do what he had to do and get to Pendle to be reunited with Emma and return Ruby's badger.

The thought of Emma and the children heading off with Saunders and the others troubled him. Joey had a nagging doubt at the back of his mind that this journey might just be a trick to get him out of the way for some reason because, as Emma said, there were so many ways Saunders' story didn't add up. But then, Ruby and Evan had dreamed of Joey too, and they had no reason to lie about it, so maybe Saunders *had* met other people; maybe at least some of his story was accurate. There was only one way to find out.

As for Emma, Joey had to trust she could look after herself.

The only reservation Joey had about sticking to the main road was the possibility he might meet other people. His belief that he, Emma and Remick—he hadn't forgotten about Remick—were the only people in the world had been dispelled, first by meeting Ruby and Evan, and then by the arrival of Saunders, Dave and Anna. There *were* other people around, and Joey didn't want to lose momentum by encountering them and having to explain everything over and over again. But for the first few miles, he saw no signs of life, the only sound that of his boots hitting the road. He had become hyper-alert to his surroundings, constantly on the lookout for movement and noises, and wondered as he walked… Had he been this aware of the world around him before? He couldn't remember.

On he went, walking and watching.

The dead rabbit was the first indication something had changed.

Of all the things Joey had encountered since he'd first found himself in this strange, empty world, the absence of birdsong was probably the eeriest. Normally, walking along a road like this, even when it was full of traffic, the hedgerows would be alive with rustling. Here, there was nothing. So when Joey saw the head of a dead rabbit protruding from under a hedge, it came as a shock, and he had to look twice to make sure it wasn't a clump of dead grass.

A clump of dead grass doesn't have ears. He cautiously approached it and nudged it with the tip of his boot.

If its presence was a shock, what came next was worse. It was not *exactly* a dead rabbit; more accurately, it was *half* a dead rabbit.

Only the upper torso, front legs and head were there. The rest had been neatly severed and was nowhere to be found.

Did something attack it? A predator or carrion bird? But no; that would have been messier. The rabbit would have been ripped apart, whereas it looked like it had been neatly cut in half with a very sharp knife, which meant—

"I know," a voice said.

Joey startled and backed away in horror, his stomach lurching as he stumbled over the person who had silently approached and was standing behind him.

"It's curious, isn't it?"

And that was how Joey came to meet Raj.

Chapter Two

THE FIRST TIME Emma saw the change come over Saunders' eyes, she was able to put it down to a trick of the light. For a second, she'd been convinced the man's eyes had ceased to be human and become something else. Something less than or—worse—more than human, his eye sockets burning with a fire that seemed to come from within. But then Saunders had turned away, not even reacting to her gasp, and when he turned back, his eyes were normal again.

Unable to contemplate the alternative, Emma put it down to tiredness and imagination. The second time it happened, it was worse, but by then, it was also too late.

The farmhouse was a flurry of activity after Joey left. Dave and Anna seemed intent on stripping it of anything useful they could carry. Saunders was in a hurry to get moving.

"Emma," he said, not unpleasantly, "could you give them a hand? We need to be gone from here."

"Are we taking another car?" Dave asked, emerging from the kitchen, munching a sandwich he had made. "Must be some good vehicles on a farm."

"No, Dave, we're walking. There are six of us now, and there may be more. I have no desire to split up."

"Why not?"

"Because I don't trust any of you. Now, hurry up. Ten minutes, then we're leaving. Emma, perhaps you could sort out the children."

Evan and Ruby had been sitting huddled together so quietly that Emma had almost forgotten they were there. *Thanks, Joey.*

Look what you've left me with. The thought of him gave Emma a strange feeling she couldn't afford to dwell on right now, so she shrugged it off. Putting on her best smiley face, she went over to the kids.

"We need to go in a minute, you guys," she said. "Come on, let's get your stuff together."

"We want to stay here," Evan said, and Ruby nodded frantically. "We're okay here."

"Can't do that, mate. We've got to go."

"We'll be okay," Evan repeated. "We can wait here for Joey. We don't like that man."

Emma glanced around to see if Saunders was listening, then leaned closer to the youngsters.

"I don't either," she whispered. "That's why I want you two to come with me. You can look after me."

"I gave Joey my badger to look after him," Ruby said with such innocence that Emma wanted to hug her.

"That's exactly why I need you," she said instead. "I haven't got a badger."

The two children looked at each other, then silently got up and went upstairs to get their things together. They were good kids, Emma had realised. Half the time she hardly knew they were there. She frowned. The thought sparked something in her mind, and she didn't know why. She ignored it and went into the kitchen where Dave and Anna were arguing.

"We don't need it, Dave," Anna was saying. "We've got enough."

"It won't take up much space," Dave argued.

"What's up?" Emma asked. She was amused to see a guilty look come over Dave's face, like a little boy caught raiding the biscuit tin.

"Dave wants to take a couple of bottles of whiskey," Anna explained.

"Just as well he isn't driving," Emma said. "Need a hand with anything? Saunders is itching to go."

"We're done here," Anna answered pointedly. Dave stormed out of the kitchen. Anna sighed. "Of all the people to get stuck with, I've ended up with him. Get yourself someone nice before you get too old to choose."

"Thanks, but I'm okay on my own."

"What about that lad Joey? He's nice."

"Joey just sort of…happened." Emma felt her face reddening. What was that about? Emma Winrush was not the blushing type. "We just ended up travelling together."

Anna grinned. "Sometimes good things 'just happen'." She looked out of the kitchen door after Dave. "And sometimes bad things do."

Emma kicked the kitchen door over with her heel and said quietly, "Honestly. What's the deal with Saunders? Do you trust him?"

"Honestly? No. There's something… But if he reckons he can get us back home, not that there's anything much there, but you know what I mean. Soon as I get back, *that* useless bag of shite is gone. It was fun for a bit, but it's time I looked after myself."

At that moment, Dave pushed the door open. "Come *on*! Have your bloody coffee morning later. We're moving out."

He heard, Emma thought. But Anna seemed unconcerned. She picked up a rucksack from the kitchen table, winked at Emma and followed Dave out of the kitchen.

Saunders was waiting in the courtyard outside the farmhouse. Evan was on one side of him and Ruby on the other, each with their own small rucksacks on their backs. Saunders was carrying nothing.

"Finally," he said. "We should be able to get a fair way in what's left of the day. Emma, you look after these two and make sure they don't lag behind. Oh, and Anna, I think I'd better look after that gun, don't you?"

He held out his hand.

With some reluctance, Anna opened her rucksack, took out the pistol and handed it over. Saunders put it in his jacket pocket.

"I think you'll feel better without it," he said.

With that, he turned and started to walk, with Dave trailing behind like a faithful puppy, the rifle over his shoulder. For some reason, Saunders had not asked for that one back. Anna followed on.

"Come on, guys," Emma said to the children. "Let's roll."

Walking behind, a child on either side and feeling uncomfortably like she belonged in *Mary Poppins*, Emma studied Saunders, who seemed to be sharing a joke of some kind with Dave. She thought of Anna's words—*there's something*—and decided to try to get closer to the other woman, make an ally of her.

That decision made what happened next all the more tragic.

Chapter Three

WHERE THE HELL did you come from?" Joey demanded, whirling around.

"Liverpool," said the young man who had seemingly appeared out of nowhere. "Just down the road. But I get asked that a lot. I think it's the accent. My parents come from Birmingham. My grandparents are from India if that helps."

Joey laughed despite himself. "That's not quite what I meant. You weren't here a minute ago."

"No." The man frowned. "That's happening a lot, too. I seem to be finding myself in a different place than I expect. It's weird. I'm Rajeev, by the way. I usually get called Raj."

"Joey," Joey replied, shaking the outstretched hand.

"Good to put a name to the face," Raj said cryptically. "I think I'm a bit like this poor bunny. I don't think he expected to be here either. I reckon half of him still doesn't."

"It's the first animal I've seen," Joey said.

"Me too. I wonder if there's a reason they can't come through."

"Come through?"

"To this reality. Wherever it is. I don't know. I'm a medical student not a quantum physicist. So, where are you headed?"

Joey felt uneasy for a moment, unsure whether he should share his purpose, but there was something likeable about this stranger, and Joey felt he could trust him.

"Back to Waterloo. That's where I've come from and it's where I'm going back to."

"That makes sense," Raj said. "I saw you with the Iron Men, but I wasn't sure if that had happened yet, if you get me?"

"No, sorry," Joey replied. "I didn't understand that at all."

Raj grinned. "Dreams. I've dreamed about you. But don't worry, it wasn't like *that*. I saw you with the Iron Men, but I also saw you at a hill, with a girl and some other people. I wasn't sure what came first."

"Neither was I," Joey answered. "But listen, I've got to—"

"Yes, I know. Things to do, places to be. Mind if I tag along? I've got nowhere in particular to be, and I'd love to hear your story."

Joey thought about it for a second, then smiled. "Okay," he said. "Let's swap stories."

As they walked, Joey told his new friend everything that had happened to him since his near miss with the BMW, right up to the moment he found the rabbit. Raj listened intently, occasionally asking questions, but mostly just listening. When Joey had finished, Raj carried on walking in silence, a look of deep concentration on his face.

"I don't like this," he said eventually. "There's too much there that doesn't add up."

"I know," Joey agreed. "I don't like any of it."

"I mean, I can kind of get what this Saunders guy means about the time repetition thing. It makes sense of a lot of things, but it doesn't explain why there are nights. Time's all wrong here, anyway, we know that, but if it's a bit of time that's just repeating, there shouldn't be night. Not unless it's a whole Groundhog Day thing."

"I think he lied," Joey said. "I'm sure of it. All that stuff about his wife and child. And all these other people he's supposed to have met. I don't know that I believe any of it, although it's a very elaborate story. Why bother?"

"Well, here's a question for you," Raj countered. "I'm sure this has occurred to you. Why you? What's so special about you?"

Joey felt a horrible sinking feeling in the pit of his stomach. It was a question he had not contemplated, had not dared to say out loud.

"I don't know," he said. "I've just kind of got on with it."

"I'll rephrase it, then," Raj said. "Why you and not someone else? If someone has to go to the Iron Men and find this key— whatever it is—why you? Why can't Saunders go himself?"

Joey shrugged. He didn't have an answer and instead asked a question of his own. "What about you? What's your story?"

"Not really very exciting," Raj replied. "I was on call at The Royal Hospital. I'd had a kip in the on-call room, and when I got up, the hospital was empty. I thought I was still asleep and dreaming for a while. Once I'd checked every ward in the place, I realised it wasn't a dream. I freaked out a bit and then I went home. There was no-one in the city centre at all, so I started walking. That was three days ago, and you're the first person I've seen since. I've just been sort of mooching about, waiting for someone else to turn up. No-one has, of course, apart from in dreams. The only sign of life was those bloody awful things that come out at night. Have you heard them?"

Joey nodded. "Seen them too."

"Rather you than me. If they look as bad as they sound…"

"Worse," Joey said with a grimace.

"Then today, I saw that half a rabbit and then you. That's it. That's my story. Told you it wasn't very exciting."

"What was that you said about finding yourself in places you weren't expecting?" Joey wanted to know.

"Yes, that's weird. I'll be in one place and then I'm somewhere else. Never far away. It's kind of like when my dad used to play some of his old LPs, you know the vinyl ones? Sometimes if one was scratched, it would jump. That's the best way I can describe it. I wondered if I had narcolepsy or something. I don't know. I mean, I've always sleepwalked, but—"

"Really?" Joey asked.

"Yeah. It's not as much fun as it sounds. Can be a bit, well, inconvenient at times. I was staying over at a friend's house one night and walked stark naked into his parents' bedroom. Scared the life out of them and outed their son at the same time. Didn't go down well. Tom dumped me a couple of days later."

Joey was briefly shocked, but then saw the grin on Raj's face and laughed. They walked on a bit further. Then suddenly Raj stopped in his tracks.

"*Listen!*" he hissed. Joey stopped too and did as he was told.

"Do you hear it?" Raj asked, frowning with concern. Joey listened hard, and sure enough, somewhere in the distance he could hear a high-pitched, unmistakable shrieking.

"But it can't be!" he gasped. "It isn't dark."

"They don't seem to care right now," Raj said. "We need to find cover."

The dual carriageway stretched out ahead and behind, with no houses that they could see. The unearthly shriek of the Screamer seemed to be coming from somewhere to their left on the other side of a small copse of trees.

"Come on!" Raj shouted and took off at a run across the road, heading in the opposite direction to the noise. Joey sprinted after him and followed Raj down a narrow lane off the main road. The Screamer was getting louder and closer, but Joey didn't dare look over his shoulder to see. He just ran. Once he nearly tripped over a pothole. It jarred his ankle, but he gritted his teeth and ran on.

Raj disappeared around a bend and Joey followed. The noise behind him was deafening, filling his head. Ahead of him, he heard a crash and the sound of wood splintering. As he rounded the bend himself, he saw Raj frantically heaving at the up-and-over door of what looked like an old garage.

"Come *on*, you bastard!" Raj shouted, but the door seemed to be stuck fast.

Joey joined him and hurled himself at the door. It felt like he had nearly broken his shoulder but the door still wouldn't shift. The Screamer was right on them now. Joey could almost feel its breath on him. Then suddenly Raj grabbed the lapels of Joey's jacket and…

…they were inside.

Joey felt a queasy lurch in his stomach, like he had just gone over the top of a roller coaster and plummeted down the other side. With the Screamer howling and battering the outside of the garage, he dropped to his knees on the grimy concrete floor, feeling like he was going to vomit.

"Yeah, I forgot to mention," Raj said. "It felt like that the first time I did it too."

"What happened?" Joey gasped. "What did you do?"

"Saved our lives. That thing out there has come for us, don't you think? I wonder who sent it."

Chapter Four

PAUL 'WEBBSY' WEBSTER often wished he could have had a cooler nickname. The rest of the crew had much better names. There was Borstal, who had done time in a YOI. Then there was Shank, because he reckoned he always went out tooled up. Lastly, there was Jimmy Six, who got his name from the number of Anfield lads he said he'd knifed.

Webbsy had been Webbsy since he was about eight or something, and it didn't matter what he did or said, he always stayed Webbsy. He thought he deserved better than that. He was as good as any of them and should get more respect than a name he'd been called since he was a kid. It wasn't Borstal or Shank who gobbed at the two bizzies who stopped their car and wanted a chat just because the lads were kicking chip wrappers into the road. It was Saturday night, for fuck's sake, and the road was full of shite anyway. So, when the car had pulled over, Webbsy and his mates had tried to play it cool. But the bizzies had got out, pulling their hats on and trying to look dead hard in their hi-viz jackets. Webbsy had got up a good mouthful, gobbed at them and legged it. He'd run down two roads before he clocked the fact he was running on his own.

His first thought was that the others had been pulled, but they'd definitely been right behind him when he started running. He paused, putting his hands on his knees to get his breath back, and looked back down the road. There was no-one. It wasn't just that the rest of the crew were nowhere to be seen. There wasn't anyone about at all. This time on a Saturday night, there were usually loads of people around, most of them staggering home, pissed and shouting. But there was nobody.

Never the brightest candle on the birthday cake, Webbsy just shrugged, went home and went to bed without noticing the house was empty. His old fella usually crashed out after the news, so the fact there were no lights on meant nothing, and Webbsy slept in until noon the next day.

The first day that Webbsy found himself alone, he was confused. It was like Christmas Day without the decorations and crap telly. He couldn't work out why there were no shoppers in the Tesco Express or Home Bargains. He walked into Tesco and walked out with a big bottle of Coke and a tube of Pringles, just because he could. Later, getting bored, he kicked in two bus shelters so he could hear how the shattering glass echoed in the street. Then he went into the offy and nicked two bottles of vodka for the sole reason that there was no-one to stop him. He emptied the cash register of money, too, stuffing handfuls of notes into his pockets. After all that, he decided he didn't want the bottles of vodka and smashed them onto one of the cars stalled empty in the middle of the road. He kept the money, though.

By the third day, he was sick of his own company and hot-wired a nice black Audi that no-one seemed to want. He drove it round, smashing into abandoned cars until it had lost both wing mirrors and something underneath was making a loud scraping noise. Then he took a silver BMW and drove to Bootle, knocking other cars out of the way like skittles as he sped along. He parked up outside the flats in Bootle where he knew Mick Lambert, the leader of one of the local gangs, lived.

Checking there was still nobody around, he went into the building, found the flat he wanted and kicked the door in, even though it wasn't locked. He took a piss on the living room carpet—to make a point—and hunted the flat until he found what he was after. Under a loose floorboard beneath a bed nobody slept in, he found a Converse trainers box. In it were two handguns, a decent supply of bullets and a stash of pills. He took all he could find and drove home.

On the fourth day, he woke up in a foul mood, He'd stolen cars, taken a slash in Mick Lambert's living room and nicked his guns, and there was no-one to witness what he had done. He dropped some speed, loaded the guns and got into his new car to go off and find something to shoot.

Chapter Five

EMMA FOUND HERSELF watching Anna. Or rather, she watched Dave watching Anna. The two weren't speaking to each other; Dave walking alongside Saunders while Anna walked on the other side, lagging slightly behind. Emma followed at the rear of the group with the children at her side. Saunders was setting a hell of a pace, and Emma had no idea how Evan and Ruby were managing to keep up; she was finding it hard enough herself. Evan had only asked to stop once, a request denied by Saunders with such venom nobody had asked since.

They had been walking for close to two hours and had just reached the village of Rufford when Dave stopped abruptly and sat down on a low wall at the side of the road. Saunders walked on for a few yards before he noticed Dave's absence and also stopped. He rounded on Dave with a fury that came from nowhere.

"What the hell are you playing at? Get up! We have to keep moving!"

"I just need a minute," Dave protested. "I think there's something in my boot."

"Then get it out and let's go!"

"Ten minutes," Anna said. "Just give us ten minutes. We've walked miles. The kids'll be exhausted."

Saunders glared at her and threw up his hands in a gesture of submission or, more likely, exasperation. "Ten minutes," he conceded. "No longer. If the children can't keep up, they can stay behind." With that, he turned his back on the group.

Emma ushered the children to the grass verge and encouraged them to sit down. She dug about in her bag and found some cereal bars which she passed around. As she nibbled hers, she watched Anna perch on the wall a few feet away from Dave. Dave, having apparently forgotten all about whatever it was in his boot, shuffled along the wall to her. She muttered something Emma didn't catch, but it clearly angered Dave because he stood up, snapped "*Bitch!*" at her and walked away to where Saunders was standing.

"Mind if I join you, guys?" Anna asked, coming over to Emma and the children. Ruby shifted to let Anna sit down, but eyed her warily.

"Thanks, Rubes," Anna said, grinning. "How are you two holding up?"

"Fine, thank you," Evan replied politely.

"He walks fast, doesn't he? Don't know about you, but I'm having a job keeping up."

"My feet hurt," Ruby complained quietly.

"Mine too," Emma agreed. "Let's rest them while we can. He'll be wanting to go again in a minute."

"Is Joey coming soon?" Ruby asked.

"Sorry, kiddo, not yet," Emma said, "He's got to do something first."

"I miss him," the girl confessed sadly. "I like Joey."

Emma was on the verge of saying 'I miss him too' but stopped herself. There was no time for those kinds of thoughts; it was quite clear Saunders and Dave were cooking something up. They were talking intently and kept looking over, but Emma wasn't sure which one of them they were looking at. Whoever they were talking about, it probably wasn't good news. Without warning, the scars on her arms began to itch.

Anna noticed her scratching, and her eyes widened when she looked at Emma's face. "You okay?" she asked.

"No," Emma said. "It shouldn't be doing that. Shush a minute."

"Why? What—"

"Anna, shut *up!*"

Anna must've realised the urgency in Emma's voice and was immediately quiet. Emma strained her ears to hear. With a horrible, sick feeling tugging at her guts, she could make out a faint, inhuman scream coming from somewhere in the distance.

"Can you hear that?" she asked Anna.

"No, what?" A confused frown wrinkled Anna's brow.

"It's one of those bastard Screamers," Emma said. "But it *can't* be. It's daylight!"

Anna listened, and Emma saw the shock register on her face. "We've got to get out of here!" she said, her voice wavering. "We've got to get inside!"

"Like where?" Emma gestured around them. "Middle of nowhere."

"What's over there?" Anna pointed to a high, ivy-clad wall on the other side of the road.

"I think it's the Old Hall." Emma had visited it during one of the few boring school trips she'd actually attended. "Mediaeval or Tudor or something."

"We need to get in there. Is there a gate?"

Emma tried to remember, but it wasn't easy with two pairs of horrified eyes staring up at her. Evan and Ruby could hear the Screamer too, and already the noise was making it hard to think.

"It's further down the road, I think, a big drive. Come on, guys." She held out a hand to the children. "We're going to have to run."

The kids got up quickly and followed Emma. Their movement caught Saunders' and Dave's attention. "Screamer," Emma shouted to them. "Can't you hear it? Come *on!*"

Without another word, Anna picked up Ruby, and Emma grabbed Evan's hand, and they took off up the road. Dave and Saunders were somewhere behind, and Emma barely had time to form the question *why aren't they hurrying?* in her mind before she saw the main gates of the hall up ahead. They were closed, but she hurtled into them to push them open. *Locked.* She collided with the gate with such force that she nearly fell over backwards, just as Anna arrived, still carrying Ruby, who was now in tears. The sickening screaming was getting ever closer, and the itch in Emma's arms was nearly intolerable.

"Every other door in this bloody world is open!" Emma snapped, banging her hand on the metal gate in frustration.

"Calm down," Anna said. "We'll have to climb over."

"Climb over?" Emma scoffed and indicated Evan and Ruby. "With these two?"

"I can climb," Evan said. "I'm good at it."

At that moment, Saunders and Dave arrived, still apparently in no hurry.

"You go first, Emma," Saunders suggested. "We'll help the children over."

Emma shot Saunders a look of resentment for turning up late to the party and taking over, but the Screamer was close now, too close, so there was no time to argue. Launching herself at the gate, she scrambled to the top, swung her legs over, dropped her bag to the ground and then followed it. Behind the group on the other side of the gate, the air shimmered and rippled. The shrieking howl was so loud she could barely hear herself yelling, "Get over NOW!"

Anna was halfway up the gate when the air tore open and the Screamer broke through in a mass of teeth as a stench like nothing she had ever smelled before filled the air. The thing paused as if weighing up its targets.

Please God, not the children, Emma prayed for the first time in as long as she could remember, but when she looked, the children, who had been huddled together by the gate, had gone. With a thump, Anna landed beside her. They could do nothing but watch as the Screamer, piece by piece, tore a shrieking, pleading Dave to shreds. One second he was there, then there was a mass of red, then he was not there any more. The rifle, which he had not had time to use, dropped to the floor with a clunk. Apparently satisfied, the Screamer disappeared, leaving a lingering odour of decay. All the while, Saunders just stood there and watched. Emma was convinced she caught a flicker of red fire in his eyes, but then it was gone.

Anna dropped to her knees on the gravel path, vomiting and crying. She repeated Dave's name in between sobs and heaves. Emma was also stunned, but not too stunned to notice that the children were suddenly back again, inexplicably on Emma's side of the gate. And Saunders…well, Saunders strolled over to where Dave had been, casually picked up the rifle and turned on them with a murderous look on his face.

It was that look that brought Emma out of her shock, and she realised, in horror, the Screamer had gone for Dave when it couldn't find the children, but it had ignored Saunders altogether.

You brought it, you bastard. You brought that thing here to kill the children.

Emma knew then that she was in far more trouble than she'd thought.

Chapter Six

JOEY AND RAJ stood like statues in the middle of the garage, barely daring to breathe with the Screamer howling outside and shaking the garage doors. Then, just as suddenly as it had arrived, it was gone. Joey let out a long breath, and his heart, which felt like it had been trying to pound its way out his chest, began to slow down.

Raj relaxed too and clapped Joey on the shoulder. "We live to fight another day. Now we've just got to figure out how to get out of here." He went over to inspect the garage door. "Locked," he said. "But then, we kind of knew that. Looks like we'll have to find something to force it."

"Can't you just jump us out again?" Joey asked.

"Nah. Doesn't seem to work like that." He started to hunt around in the gloom. "Come on, it's a bloody garage! There must be something!"

Joey joined him in the hunt. It was fairly obvious that the garage had not been used in some time and had been emptied before it had been abandoned. There was nothing in there apart from a few old bricks, or so it seemed until he heard a metallic clang as Raj kicked something by one of the walls.

"Hang on. Here we go." Raj came over to Joey carrying what looked like a filthy, rusty crowbar. "Knowing my luck, the damn thing'll be so old it will snap."

"Let's give it a go," Joey suggested.

Raj inserted one end of the crowbar under the door by the lock so that it was sticking up at an angle. He and Joey then pushed down on it as hard as they could. The door creaked but didn't move.

"Push harder!" Raj gasped.

"I am!" Joey grunted, pushing again. There was still no movement.

Joey straightened up, breathing hard, his arms aching from the effort. "Get back a minute. I'm going to stand on it."

"I don't know if that's a good idea," Raj said, but stepped away without trying to stop him.

Leaning on the door with one hand, Joey put one foot and then the other on the crowbar, forcing his weight downwards. There was nothing at first, but then Joey pushed again. With a crack, the lock gave way. Joey stumbled off the crowbar as the door shifted and landed on his backside on the garage floor, the bar smacking into his left knee on the way down.

Raj hurried over to help him up. "Nice one, Joey. You okay?"

"Think so," Joey replied, flexing his knee. "Going to have a hell of a bruise." He brushed the muck from the back of his jeans as Raj hauled the door the rest of the way up and the garage flooded with light.

"Freedom!" Raj laughed.

Despite the pain in his knee, Joey found himself laughing too. They left the garage and went out into the light, but not before Raj had retrieved the crowbar. "Think I'll take this baby with me."

"Do you want the extra weight?" Joey asked.

"I don't care. It's my lucky crowbar."

With that, they picked up their bags and started to walk.

"You know, something's just occurred to me," Raj said as he strode along, Joey limping to keep up. "Those things, Screamers, whatever they are. They just appear out of nowhere, right?"

"Right," Joey agreed. "So?"

"So why can't they come inside? You ever wondered that?"

"I hadn't thought about it," Joey confessed. "Emma just said they didn't, so…"

"Hadn't really thought about it till now. Interesting, isn't it? I wonder why. They seem to be able to go anywhere, but only outside. They're pretty useless, if you think about it. Big scary monster and you can stop it by shutting the door in its face. It's a bit like Daleks not being able to go upstairs."

"They can now," Joey pointed out automatically and then was struck by a pang. How long was it since he had been in Mr. A's newsagent looking at his *Doctor Who* magazine?

"Geek," Raj said.

"Total geek," Joey admitted. "Or I *was*."

"You will be again. All we've got to do is get you to Waterloo without being eaten, find whatever the hell it is you're looking for, get to Pendle, again without being eaten, and then we can all go home. Easy."

"Well, when you put it like that…" Joey laughed and they walked on in companionable silence.

About a mile down the road, they found the corpse.

Raj noticed it first. They were on the outskirts of Maghull, a town Joey mainly knew for the council recycling centre his dad often visited, when Raj grabbed Joey's arm and pointed to the gate of one of the houses. Joey didn't get what Raj was pointing to at first, but then saw a pair of pink trainers sticking out of the gate.

"Someone's having a kip," Raj said. "Should we wake them?"

As they drew level, Joey looked again. The trainers belonged to a woman who was lying face down and motionless across the path. She was wearing a red dressing gown, and her dark hair was spread across the ground around her head.

"I don't think she's asleep," Joey said. "She needs help."

He eased the gate open and crouched down next to the woman, his knee protesting as he did so. Tentatively, he reached out a hand and touched her shoulder.

"Are you okay?" he found himself asking but already knew there was no point. Her shoulder was a dead weight under his hand. "I think she's dead."

Raj knelt beside him, and together, they turned the woman over onto her back. She looked to be in her forties, but it was hard to tell because her pale face had the pattern of the paving stones etched into the skin. Joey was no judge, but it looked like she hadn't been dead long.

"Wasn't the Screamer," Raj said. "Look."

He parted the woman's dressing gown to reveal that the once white T-shirt she wore under it was stained with a red that was so dark it was nearly black. Through the gore, Joey could just about make out a hole which had ripped through the fabric and into the woman's chest.

"I think she's been shot," Raj said.

Joey stood up so quickly he went light-headed. *Shot?* Then he thought, *Dave had a gun.* Then only one thought filled his head.

Emma.

Chapter Seven

D AVE WAS NO threat to Emma now. All that remained of him was a dark stain soaking into the soil and a few garnet droplets of blood on the grass. Apart from that, it was only Anna's hysterical sobbing that gave any clue he had ever existed.

Anna seemed to be taking Dave's death harder than Emma had expected, bearing in mind that just before the Screamer attacked she hadn't wanted anything to do with him. But she'd started screaming when Dave had been eviscerated and had only stopped when her voice went hoarse. Emma had stood by, wanting to slap her but unable to bring herself to do it.

Now, Anna was kneeling on the ground, her arms wrapped around her body, rocking backwards and forwards and weeping with great shuddering sobs. On the other side of the gate, Saunders stood impassively to one side, his face unreadable, while on their side, Evan and Ruby huddled together, looking up at Emma with frightened eyes. *Great. What the hell do I do now?*

"Shame," Saunders said, looking at the stain on the ground that had once been Dave. "I quite liked him. He was amusing."

"*Amusing*?" Emma echoed. "He's dead!"

"Yes," agreed Saunders. "Not so amusing now. Still, it's done. Can you unlock that gate from your side? And she needs to pull herself together. We've wasted enough time here."

"Wasted…you heartless bastard!" Emma spat. "Didn't you see what just happened? Anna and the kids are in shock. No-one's going anywhere right now."

"Open the gate, Emma," Saunders repeated.

"Or what?"

"Or you can stay there. It doesn't really make any difference to me."

Emma glared at him. What she really wanted to do was climb over the gate and punch Saunders' lights out.

"See you, then," she said. "What are you going to do? Your little mate's dead and there's four of us."

"And I've got the gun. Well, I'm not sure about four of you anyway." Saunders smirked. "All I can see is one damaged girl, a hysterical mess and two idiot children. It's not what you'd call an army, is it?"

"It's enough," Emma answered, not feeling as confident as she was trying to sound.

"If you say so. I may see you at Pendle. I'll still be going there, and so will you because you'll want to see if young Joey makes it. I hope he does, although I suspect he's going to find it difficult."

"He'll get there," Emma said. "Joey will find us."

Saunders gave a dry laugh like old leaves. He crouched down by the gate near where the children cowered.

"Don't you touch them!" Emma warned.

"I just wanted to say goodbye," Saunders said, reaching through the bars of the gate to ruffle Ruby's hair. Ruby flinched violently, and she and Evan shuffled backwards out of Saunders' reach.

"Goodbye, then," Saunders said. "Be careful."

He straightened up and, without another word or look, walked off down the road. Emma watched him go and could have sworn she could hear him whistling. When Saunders was out of sight, she turned her attention back to Anna. She crouched beside the other woman and put her arms around her.

"Come on," she said. "Saunders has gone."

"I left him!" Anna cried. "I left him and they...they..."

"Shh. It's okay," Emma whispered, helping Anna to her feet. "Come on, let's see if this place has a coffee bar or something. I don't know about you, but I could do with a brew."

As Anna leaned unsteadily against her, Emma turned to Evan and Ruby. "Come on, guys. It's just us now and we're going to be okay. Let's go and see if we can find you a drink and maybe some cake. What do you think?"

Evan managed a weak smile and hurried over to Emma. Ruby lingered behind for a second and then followed. If Emma had not been preoccupied with Anna, she might have caught the look of hatred that briefly crossed Ruby's young face and the spark of red fire that flickered momentarily in her eyes.

Chapter Eight

W E SHOULD BURY her," Raj said.

Joey stood looking at him for a moment. The brain that belonged to his old life had just kicked in and informed him that dealing with the bodies of people who had been shot was not something for him to be involved in. There were other people who dealt with things like that, the police for a start.

"What?" Raj asked, seeing Joey's confusion. "We can't just leave her there."

"But someone did this," Joey argued. "Shouldn't we…"

"Wait for a copper to appear? Or an undertaker? We could be waiting a while."

"Sorry. I was just…you know…*back*. I keep forgetting we're all there is."

"Well, apart from all the other people who keep turning up. I know what you mean, though. New place, new rules. It's just a bit difficult to work out what the rules are sometimes."

Raj bent down and hooked his hands under the dead woman's armpits. Joey took hold of her ankles, and between them, they half lifted, half dragged the corpse through the open door of the house. They paused inside the hall and Raj looked round.

"Hope she's got a garden," he said. "We're in trouble if she's only got a patio."

"*I* hope she's got a spade," Joey replied and, despite the fact they were standing in a murdered woman's hall with her corpse at their feet, they both found themselves laughing.

Luckily, the house had a sizeable garden at the rear and a shed with an array of tools. Raj had to smash the shed window with a stone to get to them, but, he reasoned, it wasn't as if the owner, whose name they discovered from mail in the house was Amanda McKenzie, was going to need the shed any more. Not in the world she had left, nor in the world in which she had all too briefly found herself. It was only once he had reached in through the window and pulled out a spade that he and Joey really began to appreciate the size of the task at hand.

"We're not really going down six feet or whatever it is, are we?" Joey asked.

"Nah. We'd be here all day," Raj said. "I'd suggest we just dig enough to cover her. It's respect, really."

Taking it in turns, they dug enough soil from the well-tended rose bed to cover the body of the late Mrs. McKenzie. Joey found two lengths of cane which he tied together in a rough cross and planted it in the ground at the head of the makeshift grave. He mumbled the Lord's Prayer, which was the only one either of them could remember, and they stood in silence.

"I reckon we should look for a back way out of here," Raj said. "Let's not forget she was shot out the front."

"You don't think the shooter will still be around, do you? They'll have gone ages ago."

"Probably. But do you want to chance it?"

Joey shook his head. Without any further discussion, they gathered their belongings, climbed the fence at the back of the garden and dropped down into the alley beyond. They followed it back onto the road and continued on their way.

Three blocks away, they found further evidence of the shooter. Whoever it was had obviously had a field day in a quiet residential street. There was barely a car that didn't have at least one window shot out, and many of the houses also had broken windows.

"He's been having fun, that's for sure," Raj observed. "He must've thought it was Christmas when he actually ran into a person."

"We'd better keep moving," Joey said. "But stay alert."

They walked on, checking all round them as they went. It reminded Joey of the news footage of soldiers in Iraq or Syria, wars which would still be raging in another world. But there was no sign of life. More importantly, there was no sign of death. After a mile or so, Joey noticed Raj had stopped looking.

"I don't think he went this way," Raj said.

"I told you, Dave had a gun," Joey said. "I bet it was him."

"You could be right. We don't know he didn't pass this way. Just because they told you, doesn't mean they were telling the truth."

Joey stopped walking. "I've got to get back to Emma and warn her," he said, his voice betraying his panic.

"No, hang on, Joey. You've got this thing to do and—"

"Sod that! Emma and the kids have got a bloody psycho with them and they don't even know it!"

"Joey, *think*!" Raj urged. "Firstly, you don't know it was this Dave guy. It's a bit worrying to think how many damn guns are lying around. Secondly, from what you've said, your friend Emma is more than capable of handling herself. If you don't think that, you've got no chance with her."

"I've got no chance with her anyway," Joey replied glumly. "I really don't think I'm her type."

"So, do what you have to do. Find the way home and be the hero. That gets the girl in most stories I've read."

Joey laughed despite himself. "You win," he said. "Let's go and be heroes. Just remember I get the girl."

"Wouldn't know what to do with one," Raj answered with a grin, but then startled, as did Joey, at the loud crash from a house further along the road. Both froze.

Raj gestured towards the house, and Joey mutely nodded. Misinterpreting Joey's nod, Raj moved off, but Joey caught his arm.

"What are you doing?" he whispered.

"Going to see," Raj whispered back.

"Are you mad? What if it's the gunman?"

"What if it's not? Someone could be in trouble."

"Yes, but—"

"Joey, back in the real world, I'm training to be a doctor. I'm supposed to help people, yeah? Keep watch. I'll be back in a minute."

Joey did as Raj had asked and kept watch while Raj cautiously crept up the road. When he reached the house where the noise had come from, he stopped and beckoned Joey over. "You need to see this!"

Heart in his mouth, Joey jogged over.

The crash had to have been caused by a wheelie bin falling over because as Joey neared, he saw that beyond the fallen bin, Raj was looking at something lying on the ground—a very large, furry something that resembled a small bear. The animal was making a sound that was a peculiar combination of whimper and growl, and Joey liked neither noise very much.

"Jesus, Raj, be careful! Is that a Rottweiler?"

"Think it's a Serbian defence dog," Raj said.

"A what? I've never heard of them. Seriously? A Serbian what?"

"Defence dog. My mate's dad had one. They're great dogs if you train them properly. It looks like it's hurt, but it won't let me near. It's protecting the house."

"How the hell did it get here?"

"I wouldn't like to try and stop it," Raj answered with a slightly nervous laugh.

"You don't think it's been shot, do you?" Joey wondered.

"Hope not. I'm not sure what I'd do if it has. I'm a doctor, not a vet—I'm not even a doctor yet." He turned his attention to the dog, speaking in a quiet, calm, reassuring voice. "You're a beautiful girl, aren't you? Easy, girl. I just want to help you." He reached out a hand for the dog to sniff, his arm tense in case he had to snatch it away. The dog lifted its head from the ground, leaving a string of drool behind. Joey took a step back. The dog's mouth looked big enough to swallow Raj's head whole, and Joey really didn't like the low rumbling that was coming from its throat.

"Easy girl," Raj said again. "Let's keep nice and calm." In the same voice, and without taking his eyes off the dog, he spoke to Joey again. "She's got a wound of some kind on her flank. I'm going to try and clean it. Could you get me some water? Maybe some antiseptic if you can?"

"I don't think she'll let me in the house," Joey said.

"Try next door," Raj suggested. "We're okay here, aren't we, girl? But I wouldn't hang about."

Joey slowly backed away and then hurried to the house next door. He tried to turn the handle, but the door was locked. He had more luck with the next house along. The door opened on a first try, and Joey went inside, all the while half expecting to hear Raj start screaming behind him.

He found the kitchen at the rear and turned on the hot water tap. He knew he should really boil a kettle but didn't want to leave Raj on his own for too long. Foraging in the cupboards under the sink, he found a bottle of TCP which didn't look too old. He tipped some into the washing-up bowl and poured in hot water. There was a tea towel on the work surface, so Joey grabbed that as well.

Before picking up the bowl, the idea suddenly struck him to have a look in the fridge, and there, sitting on a plate and wrapped in cling film, was the remains of a Sunday joint of beef, the leftovers from a lunch nobody was going to return to, not in this world anyway. Joey awkwardly shoved the beef in his pocket, picked up the washing-up bowl and went back out to see if Raj still had all his limbs.

He was pleasantly surprised to see Raj sitting cross-legged on the ground, stroking the dog's large head. The dog was responding by thumping its tail on the floor.

"Her name's Misha," Raj said gently. "She's got a tag on her collar. We're friends now, aren't we, girl?"

"You'll be even better friends in a minute," Joey said, setting the bowl down next to Raj. He produced the beef from his pocket. "Look what I found."

"We might have to cut it up for her."

"If I'd had time, I'd have made some gravy," Joey joked. "Maybe a few roasties."

"It was a good thought," Raj said. Taking the beef from Joey, he unwrapped it and dug a large penknife out of his bag, using it to part cut, part tear the meat into chunks which he dropped in front of Misha. While the dog wolfed them down, he soaked the tea towel in water and set to work bathing the wound.

"Oh, she's a good girl," he cooed. "What a good girl. It's not that bad, actually. She was lucky." When he had finished, he sat next to Misha, stroking her while she ate her meal. "She should come with us," he said.

"Do you think?" Joey said, a little incredulous. "Won't she want to stay and protect the house?"

"There's one way to find out." Raj stood up. "We've got to go, Misha. It's up to you, baby. You can come with us, or stay."

He gestured to Joey with his head, and, picking up their bags, they started off up the street. As they neared the corner, they looked back. Misha was following, cautiously at first, but gradually picking up pace. By the time they had gone around the corner, Misha was trotting happily along beside them.

What they hadn't noticed was that Misha was not the only one following them. Tailing them at a safe distance was Webbsy, a gun in each hand, looking for someone else to shoot.

Chapter Nine

EMMA FOUND THE Old Hall's coffee shop without too much difficulty and made coffee for herself and tea with plenty of sugar for Anna. She let Evan and Ruby have their choice from the soft drinks in the fridge and the cakes under glass domes on the counter. The cake was slightly stale, which surprised her, but it was edible.

"Can we explore?" Evan asked.

Emma was about to say no but reminded herself she'd just loaded the kids up with sugar and calories. Besides, she wanted to talk to Anna.

"Okay," she said, "but don't go far. You see anything you don't like, come straight back, okay?"

The kids hurried off, but not before Ruby had looked Emma in the eye and given her a smile that Emma found hard to interpret, and for some reason didn't quite like. Emma ignored it for the time being and turned her attention to Anna, who was sitting at one of the coffee shop tables nursing her tea.

Emma sat down next to her. "How are you doing?"

Anna didn't look up from her tea. She also showed no signs of drinking it.

"Drink your tea, Anna," Emma prompted. "It'll make you feel better."

Anna obediently took a sip of tea, then looked up at Emma, her already puffy eyes filling with tears. "They took him to bits. I left him to be taken to bits."

Emma sighed. She'd never been much good with other people's upset, probably because, with her dad bearing his troubles in stoical silence, she had never really had much experience. *How the hell did I get to be the adult here?* "There was nothing you could do, Anna. If you'd been there, they'd have got you too."

"Might have been better." The tears spilled down Anna's cheeks.

"Now listen," Emma said firmly. "You can't think like that. It was horrible, but we survived. We have to go on surviving. I've got to look after those kids and do whatever I've got to do, but I need you with me, okay?" Anna did not respond, so Emma said it again. "*Okay?*" This time, Anna nodded.

Emma took a mouthful of coffee before she spoke again. She wanted a cigarette but had none left.

"We've got to decide what to do. I think we've got two choices. We could carry on to Pendle and wait for Joey to show up, or we could head back to Waterloo and find him."

"Saunders said we had to go to Pendle," Anna said. The tea was bringing some colour back to her face.

"Saunders said a lot of things. I'm not sure I believe any of them."

"But the dreams…I saw you at the hill. You and Joey."

"Yes, me *and* Joey. I think Saunders split us up on purpose. He's up to something. I saw…"

"What?" Anna asked, looking fearful again. "What did you see?"

"I saw something in his eyes. Might have been a trick of the light, I don't know, but there was something. I don't trust Saunders, and I don't like him."

"So what do we do?"

"I think we need to follow him to Pendle and find out what he's up to. If there's a chance we can get home, I don't want Saunders ruining it."

Until she said it out loud, Emma had still been undecided about what to do. She didn't want to tell Anna her suspicions that Saunders had somehow brought the Screamer down on them, or that he had been trying to attack the children. Anna was fragile enough. That would make her freak. But Emma had a creeping feeling that Saunders was going to have to be dealt with, and soon.

"Joey won't be far behind us," she said. "Maybe a day at the most. I think we should press on."

Before they could talk any further, they were interrupted by a scream from outside.

"Evan!" Emma yelled, leaping up so fast she sent her chair clattering to the floor. With Anna following, she ran outside.

She spotted the kids straight away. Ruby was at the top of a small flight of stone steps, and Evan was at the bottom, rubbing his leg.

Emma ran over to him and helped him to his feet. "Are you okay, Evan?"

"My leg…"

Emma rolled his trouser leg up and saw a raw patch where he had grazed his knee. It was going to be sore, and would probably bruise, but nothing serious.

"Come on, let's get this cleaned up. I think you'll live. What happened?"

"It was my fault." Ruby came down the steps to join them. "He tripped over me."

"It was an accident," Evan said. "It's okay."

"I'm sorry." As Ruby spoke, Emma caught a strange smirk on the girl's face.

No, you're not. You're not sorry. Now why would that be?

As she helped Evan trudge back to the coffee shop, she couldn't help but notice Ruby walking on ahead. Something had changed. Ruby and Evan had always acted almost as one, with Ruby deferring to her brother. Another mystery. Emma was starting to get fed up with mysteries.

Chapter Ten

WEBBSY DIDN'T THINK anything would ever feel as good as the moment he shot the woman. He'd had plenty of target practice, shooting windows and cars, but much as he enjoyed the sight and sound of the glass exploding, there was something vaguely disappointing about it. After a while, it all got a bit samey. You shot out one window, you had pretty much shot them all.

He had wandered through the streets, a gun in each hand, feeling like a gunslinger in one of those crap old cowboy movies they showed on Sunday afternoons sometimes. But without anything worth shooting at, they might as well have been the toy guns he'd had when he was little. He couldn't believe his eyes, then, when he turned a corner and saw a door opening in one of the houses. He hadn't seen a living soul in days, and suddenly a door was opening and someone was coming out. He crouched down behind a low wall and waited to see who it was.

The woman who emerged from the house, yawning and rubbing her eyes, was middle-aged and plain, which Webbsy found a bit of a downer. The first person he'd seen in days and she looked like that. He'd been hoping for someone a bit fitter. Still, it was better than nothing. He hid the guns behind his back and strolled over, all casual, like he was just out for a walk.

"Morning," he said.

The woman looked visibly shocked, like she hadn't been expecting to see anyone, and took a step back. Not wanting to let her retreat into the house, Webbsy whipped out one of the guns from behind his back and let off three shots into her chest, one after another. He'd wanted a head shot, just to see what would happen, but didn't have time to aim.

The woman was thrown backwards by the shots, hit the doorframe with her back and slid to the ground, face down. Webbsy went over to inspect his work, the gun still levelled in case he needed to finish her off, but she just lay there, twitching, making a wet gurgling sound. Webbsy pointed the gun at her head, but she twitched once more and then was still.

Webbsy stood and stared. He'd done it. He'd killed someone. He'd pointed a gun like it was the easiest thing in the world and shot another person. He wanted to shout "YES!" at the top of his voice, but stopped himself. What if someone had heard the shots? If this woman was here, were there other people around? He was still trying to learn the rules of this new world. Suddenly anxious, he took off down the road at a sprint, putting distance between himself and the woman's corpse.

He ran down two streets, seeing no-one, and would probably have carried on running if a massive dog had not launched itself at a garden gate a few streets along, barking like a lunatic and nearly making Webbsy shit himself. The dog was enormous, and Webbsy automatically pointed the gun and pulled the trigger. The dog let out a yip and Webbsy didn't wait around. He ran. Two more streets and he was able to stop and look around. He didn't know where he had hit the dog, but it wasn't following. He sat down by a wall and tried to get his breath back.

As his heart slowed down to normal, elation took over. He'd shot a person and taken down the biggest fucking dog he'd ever seen. He was unstoppable. And he wanted more.

He sat there for maybe an hour, trying to figure out what to do next, and decided he wanted to go back. He wanted to look at the woman again, maybe shoot the corpse a few times to see what would happen, so he circled the block, avoiding the street with the dog just in case. But as he approached the woman's road, he was horrified to hear voices.

Peering around a hedge on the corner, he saw two male figures, a lad about his own age and a Paki who looked a bit older, dragging the woman into the house. Webbsy's first instinct was to walk away, but something about the situation incensed him. How dare they take away *his* kill? He decided to wait for them to come out. From where he was, he could probably pick them off one at a time when they reappeared.

But they didn't come out. He waited for ages, feeling angrier and angrier. Eventually, his patience ran out, and he crossed the road to the house, entering cautiously with his guns at the ready. He stood in the hall listening, but the only sound he could hear was his own breathing. Slowly, he moved through the house into the kitchen, where he found the back door wide open. They had gone out the back, the bastards!

He went out into the garden in pursuit and was brought up short by the sight of a pile of soil in the middle of the tatty lawn with a makeshift cross planted at the head of it. In a rage, he lashed out with his foot, kicking the cross down and stamping on it until there was nothing left but matchsticks. Then, checking his guns were still loaded, he went back through the house and out into the street to find the two who had done this.

Webbsy was blind with anger as he stumbled along the road. He'd get the Paki first, he decided, and let his boyfriend watch. Maybe he'd get them with leg shots first, kneecap them so they'd know what was happening, let them see who was doing this to them before he finished them off. He'd forgotten about the dog until he saw his quarry up ahead, walking along like they were on a frigging date with the dog limping beside them. He was about to take aim, when a voice behind him said, "*No.*"

He whirled around, guns in front of him, but there was nobody there. All he could see was what looked like the vague figure of a man but seemed to be made out of smoke.

"Come out," Webbsy said, his voice wavering. "Come out, man, I'm armed."

"*I am out.*" The voice came half from the smoke figure and half in Webbsy's head. "*This is as much as I can manage. I wouldn't try shooting. You'll be wasting your bullets.*"

Webbsy stared, thinking, *I'm losing it.*

"What…who are you?" he asked.

"*My name is Saunders,*" the smoke figure said. "*At least, at the moment. I need you to come to me. I'll show you how. You're not ideal, but you'll do.*"

"I'm not going anywhere with you, man," Webbsy said, bravado taking over. "You're not real."

"*Oh, I am,*" the figure said. "*And you will come with me. You'll come with me, and I'll give you plenty to shoot at.*"

Chapter Eleven

JOEY, RAJ AND Misha walked on undisturbed for several miles, blissfully unaware they had been followed for a while. Their paths would cross with Webbsy's again, and this time they would meet face-to-face, but not until Pendle. For now, Joey and Raj chatted as they walked, and Misha trotted alongside, walking more easily now and more often on Raj's side than Joey's.

For his part, Joey had forgotten his misgivings about getting involved with a dog of that size and enjoyed Misha's company every bit as much as Raj did. It seemed strange to be able to throw a stick for a dog down the middle of a main road and allow the dog to run free to retrieve it, but as with everything else, he adapted quickly.

One of the reasons Misha may have stayed loyal to her new friends was that she was very well fed. Not having a tin opener with them, there was no tinned food for her. Instead, she was fed on cooked meats from shops they passed along the way. It was at one such shop, a large supermarket on the way to Crosby, that Raj noticed the same thing Emma had. He opened a packet of cooked chicken and was about to offer a chunk to Misha when something made him sniff the meat.

"Does that smell okay to you?" He handed the packet to Joey, who sniffed warily and frowned.

"I don't know. It's not quite right. It's probably okay for Misha, but I wouldn't eat it."

"That's what I thought," Raj said. "And isn't that a bit odd? I thought the rules of this place were that things don't go off. Nothing has so far. Why now?"

Joey pulled a face. "Haven't a clue."

"I haven't, either," Raj conceded. "I don't like it."

They picked up some snacks for themselves and a packet of dried dog food for Misha and headed on their way. Half an hour later, they were close to their destination.

"So," Raj said, "lead me to these Iron Men."

"It's not far," Joey told him.

"You know, considering I've lived in Liverpool a couple of years now, I've never seen them. They worth seeing?"

"I suppose so. I'm used to them. They're just *there*, you know? I haven't got a clue what I'm supposed to be looking for, though."

"Let's hope we know it when we see it."

Joey led Raj down a long, tree-lined road past some very large, very expensive houses, some of which were hidden behind security gates.

"Footballers," Joey explained. "Not many other people can afford them."

"I'll tell you what, if we don't find a way home, I'm coming back here to live. I quite fancy living like a footballer."

Joey laughed but was troubled by the serious point that lay underneath Raj's joke. "Do you think that's possible? That we won't get home, I mean."

"You tell me," Raj said. "You're the hero."

Joey laughed again, but this time ironically. "If I knew what I was supposed to do…"

"You'll find out soon enough."

Before they could get any further, however, they found that their route was blocked by a railway level crossing. Joey knew the crossing well; his father had often been held up here. Frequently, trains travelling in both directions had to be allowed to pass before the barriers could be raised. Right now, the barriers were down and an eerily empty train was frozen halfway across. To get over the crossing, they had to resort to the footbridge, which seemed simple enough, except that Misha was strangely reluctant to set foot on it.

"Come on, girl," Raj cajoled. "Good girl. It's only a bridge."

But the dog would not budge. Raj stood on the first few steps of the bridge, slapping his thigh and encouraging her, but she sat firmly at the bottom and would not move.

"Could have done with picking up a lead from somewhere," Joey remarked, earning an unusually filthy look from Raj.

"Obviously doesn't like bridges," he replied, coming back down off the bridge and stroking Misha affectionately on the head. "Let's see if she likes this any better."

He took a short run and vaulted over the level crossing barrier.

"Come on, girl!" he called. "Come on, Misha!"

Tail wagging, and with a short *woof*, Misha followed, taking one huge leap over the barrier. It was a great game to her, and when Raj ran around the stationary train and vaulted the barrier on the other side, Misha enthusiastically followed.

Joey thought about using the bridge himself but decided not to look like a wimp in front of Raj. Just as his friend had done, he took a short run and half jumped, half climbed over the first barrier. He crossed the tracks and went around the front of the train, where he could see Raj playing with an excited Misha on the other side.

"At least we know she wasn't too badly hurt!" Raj called. "Come on, Joey! Get a move on!"

It was probably because Raj was rushing him that Joey lost concentration. But whatever the reason, when he tried to jump the second barrier, his foot caught in the rail, and he pitched, face-first, onto the road beyond. It might not have hurt quite so much if he hadn't put his hand out to break his fall, but he felt his right wrist turn as he hit the ground and sat there in a heap, feeling like an idiot, but worse, feeling like he might have broken his wrist.

Raj came over to check on him. "You okay? You were supposed to go over it, not through it."

"I'm fine," Joey lied. "It's just my wrist."

"Let's have a look." Raj squatted down next to Joey and felt all along the offending wrist. Pain shot up Joey's arm, causing him to suck in air through his teeth.

"The good news is it's not broken. You've probably sprained it. We could do with getting hold of something to strap it up."

"Later," Joey said, picking up his bag with his good hand and slinging it over his shoulder. "Let's go."

"You sure?" Raj asked. "It's going to hurt like a bastard."

"I'll be fine," Joey said, heading off down the road. "Let's do what we've got to do."

Raj and Misha followed him, and within a few minutes they'd reached the coast. They crossed a car park and found themselves on a sand-covered coastal path. Joey leaned against a metal rail which seemed to run for miles in either direction. He could taste the tang of salt in the air.

"It's weird. There's usually seagulls everywhere. Anyway, there they are." Joey gestured. "That's the Iron Men."

The deserted beach would have presented an uncanny enough sight as it was, but with the dozens of man-shaped figures dotted along it was disturbing. They stood, buried in sand to one height or another, with their blank, sightless faces pointing out to the Mersey, as if watching for ships that would now never come.

"I don't much like that," Raj said with a shudder. "It looks… *odd*."

Then one of the figures moved, causing Raj to swear and step back, nearly stumbling over Misha, who was sitting right behind him.

As the figure started to walk up the beach towards them, it rapidly became apparent that it was not like the others. This one was made of flesh and blood. It was wearing a worn leather jacket, and its straggly hair was being whipped by the sea breeze.

"I know who that is," Joey said, his heart sinking. "His name's Remick."

Chapter Twelve

B Y THE TIME they were all ready to leave the Old Hall, Emma had more or less forgotten any suspicions she might have had about Ruby. Evan had a nasty graze to one knee, which Emma had bathed, but seemed fine otherwise. He still insisted his fall was entirely his own fault; he'd been looking the other way and simply tripped over his own feet.

Anna was quiet and withdrawn. Although she was no longer as shaken as she had been directly following Dave's death, she was firm in her belief that she was to blame, and nothing Emma said could change her mind.

Emma was uncomfortable with other people relying on her. She wasn't used to this. She was perfectly happy looking after herself; indeed, that was how she preferred it to be. At least when Joey was there, it diluted the responsibility. Even if they didn't always agree, they discussed things. Her every instinct screamed at her to leave the kids with Anna and head off on her own, but she knew, realistically, that was the last thing she should do. But they needed to get moving, and quickly. She didn't want to be delayed so much that Joey did whatever it was he had to do and got to Pendle before her, especially if Saunders got there first.

"Are you ready?" she asked Anna.

"I suppose so. We're not doing any good here." She put her jacket on, picked up her bag and headed for the door to the coffee shop.

"Okay, kids," Emma said, surprised by Anna's eagerness to leave, "looks like we're on the move again."

***

Evan quickly picked up his own small bag and made sure Ruby had gathered her belongings together. His knee was still very sore where he had scraped it on the step, but it felt a bit better after Emma had bathed it. He hadn't been too sure about her at first. Joey had been the nice one when they first met. Emma was the scary one who didn't really want anything to do with them. But things had changed when the other people had arrived at the farmhouse. She was still fierce, but at least Evan and Ruby knew she was on their side. Since Joey had left—Evan really, really hoped he would be back soon—Emma had started looking after them properly, and Evan liked her now.

Of course, Emma didn't know Evan was perfectly capable of looking after himself, and Ruby too. Back in the other world, he had been very good at not being noticed. His stepfather worked very long hours and liked peace and quiet when he came home. The last thing he needed was the noise made by two young children. If they made too much noise and disturbed him, he was very capable of lashing out with slaps. So Evan tried to be as quiet as he could and just not be noticed.

The first time he realised he could actually vanish and not be seen at all was when he and Ruby had run away from the thieves in the supermarket. The bad people had run after them, but out in the car park, they'd looked right at Evan and Ruby and couldn't see them. The children could see each other, clear as anything, but it was like they had become invisible to anyone else.

He'd practised a bit more when Mr. Saunders and the other two arrived. He really didn't like the way Mr. Saunders looked at him and Ruby, so he concentrated hard on not being seen. Mr. Saunders looked a bit confused when it happened but had a lot of other things on his mind.

It was when the screaming thing with all the teeth attacked them that Evan realised the value of his newfound talent. He could see the thing coming and just knew it was coming for him and Ruby. Without thinking too hard about it, he'd grabbed hold of Ruby's hand and made them vanish, and the thing with the teeth had killed that other man instead. Evan and Ruby had managed to squeeze through the bars of the gate, and still nobody could see them. Evan felt bad that the other man had been killed, but it was his job to look after Ruby, so that was what he had done.

But now, after years of looking after Ruby, she suddenly didn't seem to want it any more. Like when they'd been playing on the stone steps, he'd wanted to show her something—he couldn't even remember what—and she'd spoken to him in a way he'd never heard her speak before.

"Go *away*, Evan!" she'd snapped, sounding more like a grown-up, and pushed him hard in the chest. That was why he'd tumbled down the steps, but even then he'd tried to protect her by saying he tripped.

He wanted to talk to Emma about it, but as they set off on their travels again, Ruby wouldn't leave his side. She didn't speak to him, but wouldn't leave him alone with Emma either. She just walked along, glancing sideways from time to time, her voice mouthing words Evan couldn't hear.

***

Emma was glad to see Evan and Ruby walking along together. She'd been worried something had happened between them, and she didn't have the time or the energy to sort it out. But they were walking along, side by side, as they always did, just a few paces ahead. *I'll never understand kids*, she thought, while still resolving to keep an eye on them.

***

Ruby was talking to the voice in her head. She didn't know who the voice belonged to, but it had appeared there after the horrible thing had attacked them. The voice told her things, *secret* things, and made her feel better. She'd been very scared after the thing had attacked them, but the voice made her feel stronger. She still felt scared, too, because the voice was sometimes nasty to her if she didn't do what she was told, but she felt like she was stronger and braver than her brother, and she liked it.

– *We're walking again*, she said.

~ *Did you hurt the boy? Can he walk? Is he slow?*

– *I tried. But he can walk.*

~ *Then try again*, the voice said. *Try harder. You know what will happen if you don't.*

– *I know.* Even in Ruby's mind, she sounded like she was going to cry.

~ *I'll hurt you, girl. And you know I can. Do you want me to hurt you?*

– *No!* Ruby cried in her head, nearly crying out loud. *Please don't hurt me!*

~ *Then do as I ask. If you don't want me to hurt you, then you must slow the boy down.*

Chapter Thirteen

REMICK WAS THE last person Joey had expected to see on Crosby beach. He hadn't really expected to see Remick again after he and Emma had left Waterloo. At the back of his mind, he'd believed Remick had sent them on some wild goose chase to get rid of them. And yet here he was, walking towards him, beckoning eagerly.

"Joey!" he called. "Come down onto the beach. Bring your friend."

Joey looked at Raj, who shrugged. They descended from the sea wall using a set of stone steps which was half hidden by drifts of sand. Misha bounded down the steps, obviously delighted by the freedom the beach offered. Remick met them at the bottom of the steps and promptly started back towards the nearest of the metal statues.

Joey and Raj followed. When they reached the statue, Remick stopped and turned to them, smiling.

"I'm pleased to see you," he said to Joey. "You too, Raj. Not sure about the dog, but that's a personal thing. Yes, I do know your name, Raj. I'll explain everything in a minute. Just come a little closer to our iron friend here."

Joey noticed straight away that this was a rather different Remick from the one he'd met previously. He looked…well, healthier was the first thing that came to mind. Whereas before he had been pale and drawn, his face now had colour to it, and he seemed younger. Gone, too, was the lingering smell of alcohol.

"You must be full of questions," Remick said. "It's difficult to know where to start."

"How about, what am I doing here?" Joey asked. "What have I come to find? Do you know where it is?"

"The key," Remick replied. "The key to unlock this world and send you home. That's what *he* said, didn't he?"

"Is it true?" Raj asked. "We know he lies."

"In a way, yes, it is true. But yes, he does lie. Often. I've been following you, my friends. I know what you've been told, and there are elements of truth in it."

"Following us?" Joey demanded. "How?"

Remick laughed and leaned against the iron man statue. "Not literally. Not physically. It wouldn't be wise for me to leave here. But there are other ways. I know about some of the difficulties you've had, but I'm afraid it was all necessary. The right things have to be in the right places, you see."

"I don't see," Joey said, feeling anger rising in him. "You told us to go to Pendle. If this bloody key—or whatever it is—was here all the time, why did we leave at all?"

"Because the children weren't here. Raj wasn't here. Anna wasn't here, or Dave. They all have their part to play, although whatever Dave's was, he won't be playing it any more..."

"Why not? What's happened to him?"

"Screamers got him. It's probably just as well. He had become Saunders' pet. Anyway, all the others are still there, but you had to leave here to find them and bring them into play. It's best if we start from the beginning. Where exactly do you think you are?"

"We've theorised it's some kind of parallel world," Raj said. "We thought it was maybe caught in some kind of repeating cycle? But it's just a theory and there are holes in it."

"Yes, quite big ones. You're sort of right. I know some of this has come from *him*, the one who calls himself Saunders. But don't forget—he lies, and with good reason. Everything he told you about his life before was a fabrication. But then, he couldn't really tell you the truth. You would never have believed it. Not everything was a lie, though. This *is* a world parallel to yours. That much is obvious. But that is about all that was true. His name isn't Saunders, either, but you probably worked that one out for yourselves."

"Who is he, then?" Joey asked.

"Best not to name him," Remick said. "Names have power, and at this stage, that really isn't a good idea."

"You make him sound like a demon, or something," Raj observed.

Before Remick could reply, they were interrupted by Misha bounding over carrying what was not so much a stick as a small branch. She dropped it at Raj's feet and sat looking up at him, panting. Raj picked it up and threw it as far as he could. With a lump of wood that size, it was not as far as he might have liked.

"I'm not sure what your beliefs are," Remick said as Misha loped off after the stick, kicking sand all round as she ran. "But, yes, you're right. Saunders is what you would call a demon."

Joey and Raj stared at each other, and then at Remick.

"That's ridiculous," Raj said. "Come on, Joey. I think we're done here. He's taking the piss."

"Why is it ridiculous?" Remick asked, holding up his hands. "You've been brought to a version of your world that has no people in it. That's ridiculous. You've been attacked by things that just appear out of the air and seem to be mainly teeth. That's ridiculous. Whether you admit it or not, you all have powers that you didn't have before. It's all ridiculous, Raj. But it's also true. Saunders *is* a demon. So am I."

Raj turned and started to walk away. "No. That's it. Misha! Come on, girl! Sorry, Joey, but if you believe this bollocks, you're on your own."

"Pity," Remick said. "I credited you with more of an open mind than that."

"An open mind?" Raj spat, whirling round and walking back to Remick so that they were face-to-face, toe-to-toe. "Have you any idea how close I am to losing my mind? Nothing here makes sense, nothing! It's all I can do to keep it together, and now you're telling me there are demons all over the place! For your information, Remick, I have a very open mind, but things like that…"

His voice tailed off, and he stared, open-mouthed, at Remick, who was no longer dressed in leather and denims but was swathed in a cloak constructed of what appeared to be flame. His hair was no longer black, but a burning red, and his eyes were glowing embers. He was also hovering roughly a foot above the sand.

"I'm sorry," he said, and his voice sounded like nothing Raj or Joey had ever heard before. "But you did ask."

Chapter Fourteen

SINCE WITNESSING DAVE being torn to shreds in front of her, Anna had been plagued by guilt. He hadn't been much of a man in many ways, but he'd been fun company while they were drinking and an adequate lover when Anna had been experiencing a drought of such things. Once Saunders came on the scene, though, Dave had changed. He'd followed Saunders like a faithful puppy and treated Anna like a servant. She'd been in relationships like that before and had no desire to go back to that. All the same, Dave didn't deserve to die the way he had. Nobody did, and if Anna could have prevented it, she would have done.

Now, all she wanted was to get back to the world she knew and pick up the pieces, if there were actually any pieces left to pick up. That was why she stuck with Emma and the kids. They weren't bad people and certainly seemed like Anna's best shot at getting home. That, of course, was if there was any truth at all in Saunders' stories, and she was starting to think ahead. If they were stuck here forever, she'd go off on her own and find somewhere quiet. She'd flitted from relationship to relationship all her adult life, and all had been unsuitable. Maybe it was time for her to have a go at living on her own, in whatever world she had to do it.

***

Emma sensed the deep sadness still tormenting Anna. As they walked, she tried to make conversation, and Anna did her best to join in, but her heart wasn't in it. Short of chatting to the kids, it left Emma feeling isolated. Back in the real world, she had few friends, but there was always human contact, even if it was the false, illusory friendships on social media.

She hadn't known she could be lonely until now, and it was all down to Joey. She missed him and was beginning to realise how much communication she took for granted back in their world. You missed someone, you messaged them or texted them or even rang them. Here, if you missed someone, you had to wait for them.

On they walked. Road signs showed that Preston was twelve, then ten miles away. From what Emma knew, they had to go through Preston, and Pendle was somewhere on the other side.

Although her legs were getting tired and her feet were killing her, there was something about walking in the open which was reassuring. Free of exhaust fumes, the air was fresh and clean, and the weather was fine. In fact, the weather was always fine here. It never seemed to rain much, and yet the plants weren't dead. Another little mystery of this world. But the sky was beginning to darken, and night was on its way. The children were complaining of being hungry, or Evan was. Ruby was still quiet, and Emma worried about the effect all this might be having on her.

"I think we should find somewhere to stop for the night," she said. "Get something to eat and have some rest. We need to be inside after dark, just in case those things come back."

And that was another odd thing. Since Dave's death, Emma had not felt the slightest itch from her scars. She didn't want to contemplate why it might be that the Screamers suddenly appeared during the day, just the once, with no sign since. She had also been walking for quite some time without even thinking about smoking. But now she had thought about it, she realised she didn't want to smoke, probably wouldn't be bothered if she never had a cigarette again. If all it took to give up was to come to another world, she'd have done it ages ago.

Half a mile or so later, they came across a pub by the side of the main road, which advertised that it was also a hotel. The door was open, and Emma suggested it would make a good base for the night. Nobody disagreed, and they all trooped inside where she let the kids go and pick their own room while she and Anna investigated the kitchen to see what they could rustle up to eat. The kitchen freezers were well stocked, and soon there were burgers sizzling on the griddle and chips going golden in the fryer.

They all sat in the small restaurant area and ate their meal, mostly in silence. The only occasion it was broken was when Ruby accidentally knocked a glass of juice off the table and Emma had to sweep up the broken glass and dispose of it. The rest of the time, Emma was aware that Anna kept glancing at the bar.

When the meal was over, and Emma had made sure the children were settled for the night, she wasn't surprised to find Anna sitting in the hotel's bar area with a bottle of wine and a glass in front of her.

"I haven't decided whether to open it," she said when Emma joined her. "If I open it, I'll drink it."

Emma took another glass from behind the bar and sat next to Anna. "Why don't I help you with it? I'm not legal, but I don't think anyone's going to card me."

Her comment produced the first laugh Emma had heard from Anna, and it was a good sound. Anna opened the bottle and poured herself a generous glassful. She started to pour wine into Emma's glass, but Emma stopped her when it was only half full.

"I'm not really used to it," she said. "My mother liked a drink but I never bothered."

"I think I like it too much," Anna admitted. "This is a one-off. I just could do with it, you know?"

"Won't do you any harm."

Anna drank her wine in several goes and poured another; Emma sipped hers.

"Do you think we'll ever get home?" Anna asked eventually.

"Honestly? I don't know. I hope so. There are just…too many lies going round. I don't know what's true any more. I guess we'll find out tomorrow."

"It'll be strange going back. How can we just go back and pick up our old lives after this?"

"Joey said there were posters up about me, saying I was missing," Emma remembered. "It'll be a bit of a shock for everyone when I just turn up again. I'm not sure how I'll explain it."

"Just say you were kidnapped by aliens or something," Anna said with another laugh, obviously mellowed by the wine.

"It isn't much stranger than the truth." Emma laughed too. "No-one will believe me either way."

Their conversation was interrupted by a noise from the kitchen. Emma put a finger to her lips and crept quietly out to investigate. "You okay, Rubes?"

The little girl was standing in the middle of the room and looking decidedly guilty. "I want a drink of water," she said, but there was a defiance in her eyes which Emma had not seen before.

"Okay. Get yourself one and then back to bed. There's a lot more walking tomorrow."

Ruby poured herself a glass of water and, without another word, left the kitchen. Emma listened as the sound of small footsteps receded up the stairs, and returned to the bar.

"Just Ruby," she said.

There was no answer. Anna was still sitting where Emma had left her, but seemed to be dozing, glass in hand. Emma carefully took the glass from her and shook her shoulder. Anna woke with a start.

"Come on," Emma said. "I think it's time we all called it a day."

Once in her own room, she lay down on the bed, wondering if sleep would come. It surprised her by coming quickly and dreamlessly.

***

In a room just down the corridor, Ruby was still awake.

– *I've done it.*

~ *I hope you have done it well,* the voice in her head replied. *Now sleep.*

***

No Screamers came that night. The screaming came in the morning, from Evan and Ruby's room. It woke Emma, who rushed into the children's room to find Evan sitting on the edge of his bed, dressed and with one trainer on.

"Evan! What's happened?"

"My foot!" Evan sobbed, tears streaming down his face.

Emma crouched down and lifted Evan's foot onto her knee. The sides of his trainer had a dark, damp stain on it, and he winced as Emma gently removed the shoe, his face contorted in pain. It didn't take Emma long to see the cause of the pain. Blood was pouring from an inch-long gash in the flesh of Evan's instep. Sticking out of the cut was a jagged shard of glass.

"How did that get in your shoe?"

"I don't know," Evan cried. "It hurts!"

Ruby, sitting on her bed and watching, said something which Emma would only later think was curious.

"It wasn't me."

"What's happened?" Anna burst into the room with her hair all over the place and her eyes blurry from sleep.

"Have a look." Emma gestured at Evan's foot. "I don't think we'll be walking very far today."

Chapter Fifteen

"THERE ARE," REMICK said, "higher powers than you know."
He had abandoned the flames and the cloak and regained his more familiar form. It had happened so quickly that Joey was now half convinced he had imagined the whole thing.

"Religion tries to put names on them, but religion is limited by human imagination. Once, there were gods created for everything humankind didn't understand; the sun, the weather, the tides. Most things have now been explained by science, but there are still some unimaginable truths."

"Are you talking about God, here?" Raj asked. "Because I've never been much of a believer. If you work in a hospital A&E department and see dying children brought in, you kind of lose your belief."

"God is one name for it. Allah is another. Other people have used Odin or Zeus or Tian. The highest power really hasn't got a name. It doesn't need one. It just *is*. But underneath that power is another hierarchy. The nearest analogue that you would understand is to call us demons. The stories about falling angels are partially right, though that is a bit simplistic."

"So, are you a good demon?" Joey asked. "I'm guessing Saunders isn't. I'm also guessing all that stuff about having to get drunk to have visions was a lie too."

"Not a lie, Joey. More of an act for your benefit. Though I have to say, I do rather like the stuff. It doesn't actually affect me...I suppose you can't have everything. Anyway, you you asked a question. Good and evil are not as black and white as you imagine. There are a great many shades in between. But for us to move on, in simple terms, yes. I am good and Saunders is evil. Though maybe malicious is a better word, cruel.

"Now, another thing you need to understand is that the highest power created your world, although, again, created is perhaps not the best word. It *caused* your world to be. And it is a brilliant creation. It's a beautiful thing. The one mistake was to allow humankind to come into being. Some people like to view the creator as some kind of puppet-master, pulling the strings of humans. To use your example, Raj, you lost belief because you could not understand why God would allow some of the things you have seen.

"But the truth is, humans were given the greatest gift when you were brought into being. You were given freedom. All the ills in your world have been caused, in one way or another, by people. Yes, sometimes Saunders and others like him might prod and poke a bit, but most of the damage that has been caused to your world, has been brought about by the greed and selfishness of its inhabitants."

"I think we know that," Raj said. "Or, at least, anyone with a conscience knows it."

"I hope so," said Remick. "But I mention it because it is relevant. When it became apparent humans were intent on destroying their planet, some of the higher, more powerful of my kind devised a plan to deal with it. They started to experiment with making a new world, a world devoid of people. That way, if you lot succeeded in wrecking your world, the worthier of your kind might be saved."

"A backup," Joey said. "You were making a backup."

"That's a good analogy, Joey," Remick said with a smile. "I like that."

"Worthier?" Raj interrupted. "And who, exactly, was going to decide which of us was worthy and which of us wasn't?"

"It never actually got as far as that," Remick replied. "There was a problem. Even the most powerful found they did not possess anywhere near the ability of the creator. They could only create small versions of the world, snapshots almost. These worlds were created with stolen time. They took the time between time, the split second between heartbeats, and fashioned new time-streams. But they were not strong enough to steal sufficient time to complete the time-streams, and the whole idea was abandoned. But the pocket worlds they had created still exist. They are there between seconds, between heartbeats."

"How, exactly, do you steal time?" Raj demanded.

"Well, *you* can't, of course, but there are those of my kind who have a responsibility over time and can more or less take what they want. By taking it from between seconds, they simply took time nobody was using, so it was never noticed. And they found an ideal use for the pocket worlds they created. They make perfect prisons for individuals like Saunders, who are not safe to roam free."

For a moment or two, there was silence as the enormity of what Remick was describing sank in.

"He's trying to escape," Joey said. "That's it, isn't it? He's trying to escape."

"You're very perceptive, Joey. And, once again, you are correct. The fact is, he simply should not be able to. The locks that were put on this place should be impregnable. No-one should be able to get into this world, and nobody should be able to get out."

"We got in," Joey pointed out.

"Yes. But as yet, we can only theorise as to how. I think it has to do with your heart, Joey. I think the irregular heartbeat you were born with has connected you with this world, possibly others. It's like when you listen to music. Some people only hear the beat. Some people can hear the syncopated beat. You're not the only ones. There are small numbers of people all over this world. We don't know how they got here, but their presence is making this world unstable.

"Time is not running correctly. It should, in theory, just be one cycle of day and night repeated over and over, but something is happening that we don't understand, and time has started to move on. You noticed that food is beginning to degrade. There are instances of animals coming through—not just your large friend there. None of this should be possible."

"Why is it now?" Raj asked. "I mean, if this world was created so long ago, why isn't the 'snapshot', as you call it, of then? Why is it now?"

"Time renews," Remick said. "Time moves on, even stolen time, and it is one thing no-one can control."

"I don't understand where we come in," Joey said. "Why is everyone dreaming about me? What am I supposed to do? What's it got to do with these statues?"

"The statues haven't actually got anything to do with it," Remick said. "They just serve a purpose. While we are here, we can talk without Saunders being able to see or hear."

"It's because they're iron, isn't it?" Raj asked. "I read somewhere that demons are vulnerable to iron. Is that actually true?"

"Nobody's perfect," Remick answered. "We all have our weaknesses."

"That doesn't answer my questions," Joey said.

"I know. And I wish I could. Somehow, *you* are the key to it all, Joey, and we don't know how. You have all acquired abilities by coming here. You must have noticed that. But we must assume that your powers are the strongest, Joey. You saw off those things Saunders sent after you. They are minor demons, by the way. They are the basis for the legends you have of what you call banshees. You should not be able to fight them, and yet you did."

"I don't know what I did," Joey said apologetically. "I don't know if I could do it again."

"I'm sure you can do surprising things when you have to," Remick said. "And you *will* have to. You are crucial in all this. That's why I have done what I can to engineer things so that you are in the right place at the right time. Saunders is not as strong as he has been and, at the moment, can't see beyond the glamours I have used to disguise myself, but he has identified you as having an important role in all this. I think he wants to use you to break free from this world, and that cannot be permitted. Oh, and one minor thing, hardly worth mentioning, really. If Saunders escapes, this world may well lose its purpose and cease to be. You really don't want to be here when that happens."

"*Minor point*?" Joey was horrified.

"Sorry," Remick said. "When you have met as many mortals as I have, you learn sarcasm quite quickly."

"Hang on," Raj interrupted. "This doesn't make sense. If you and the others of your kind have the power to make a world and imprison Saunders in it, why can't you do something about it? You're the ones with the powers. As you were good enough to remind us, we humans aren't quite in your league."

"It's a good question," Remick said, "and not an easy one to answer. I said earlier that among my kind there are hierarchies. Those hierarchies are very complex and rely on very old alliances, accords and agreements. It means that the balance is very delicate. Those alliances have been in place for millennia. In short, we all just get on with what we are doing. Too much interference can tip the balance. To put it as simply as I can, we don't want to start a war. It would be a war nothing would survive."

Chapter Sixteen

IT WAS UNLIKELY Evan was going to be walking anywhere in the immediate future. The position of the wound was such that there was no way he could walk without putting pressure on it. It was bleeding badly and very painful. There was also the small matter of the piece of glass sticking out of it.

"We need to take that out," Emma said to Anna. "I don't know what I'm doing here."

"I do," Anna replied. All traces of the guilty, fearful woman were gone and the former nurse took over. "Emma, have a look round for a first-aid kit. It's a pub, it must have one. Maybe in the kitchen. I need hot water and paper towels, too. If I need to, I can stitch it, but I need a good look at it first."

Without questioning, Emma ran downstairs to the pub kitchen and scouted around for a green box. She found one near the door and opened it. It seemed well-equipped, as far as she could tell. There were dressings, wipes and even a small bottle of disinfectant. She ran water until it was as hot as she could stand and poured some into a small mixing bowl. Tucking a large roll of kitchen towel under her arm, first-aid kit in one hand and bowl in the other, she raced back upstairs as quickly as she dared.

In the bedroom, Anna and Evan were sitting on the bed. Anna had the boy's foot raised on her knee. Ruby was standing by the window watching with a look on her face which, to Emma, betrayed no concern at all for her brother. Emma pushed that thought out of her head for a moment while she organised the supplies for Anna.

Anna nodded her thanks and dampened some kitchen towel. "Okay, my brave boy. Let's have a proper look. I'm just going to bathe it, so it may sting a bit. Is that okay?"

"Yes." Evan's voice wavered with anxiety and pain.

"Good lad." Anna dabbed at the wound with the dampened towel. It came away red. "That's not as bad as it looks," she told Evan, but the look she gave Emma said something completely different. "I need to get that glass out. It's not very deep, but it is going to hurt, Evan. I'm sorry."

"It's okay. Do what you need to."

"That's my boy," she praised and took a pair of tweezers out of the first-aid kit.

"Hold my hand, Evan," Emma said, taking his small hand in hers. "Squeeze if you need to."

Anna dampened some more kitchen roll with one hand and with the other took hold of the shard of glass and pulled. Evan winced, but he didn't pull his foot away as Anna pressed the wad of kitchen towel hard to his instep. Frowning, she withdrew her hand and shook it.

"What's the matter?" Emma asked.

"Nothing. Just pins and needles." Anna dismissed Emma's concern and smiled at Evan. "That's the worst bit, sweetheart. Now we just need to stop the bleeding and get it dressed. Could you do me a favour, Evan? Could you hold this towel where it is? You'll need to keep holding it tight. Can you do that?"

Evan nodded grimly and took over holding the wad of towel to his foot. Anna led Emma out of the room and closed the door over.

"How is it?" Emma asked.

"Bad. That glass was deeper than I thought, and it's a nasty gash. If the bleeding doesn't stop, he could really do with stitches. Whatever, he's going to have to stay off it."

"So we're not going anywhere," Emma stated flatly. "Great."

"Let's get it dressed and see. How the hell did glass get in his shoe, anyway?"

"Beats me." In her mind, Emma heard Ruby saying 'it wasn't me'.

"If you need to get on to Pendle, leave them with me," Anna suggested. "We'll follow on when we can."

"Let's just see," Emma said. "But thanks."

They went back into the room where Ruby hadn't moved from the window and Evan was still dutifully clutching the pad to his foot.

"Right, let's have a look." Anna took the pad from Evan and peeled it away. "What the—" She'd clearly stopped herself from swearing. "Emma, you need to look at this."

Emma leaned over Anna's shoulder and nearly swore herself. "That's just... What *is* that?"

"That," Anna said, staring incredulously, "is what we in the medical profession would call a miracle."

The cut, which had been leaking blood uncontrollably, was now no longer bleeding. Anna unwrapped a sterile wipe from the first-aid kit and cleaned the dried blood from the base of Evan's foot. The cut looked slightly damp, but it could have been moisture from the wipe. Otherwise, it looked like it was already partly healed.

"It doesn't hurt any more," Evan said. "What did you do?"

"I think it's you," Anna replied. "I think you're Wolverine."

Evan laughed, and Emma could tell it was genuine. He really wasn't in pain any more. Anna carefully dressed the base of Evan's foot and helped him up. Evan gingerly placed his bare foot on the floor and slowly put weight on it. He beamed at Anna. "It's fine. Honestly! You've cured me!" He hugged her. She couldn't help but grin herself.

Emma looked over at Ruby, who was the only person not smiling. *You really don't like that, do you?* Emma thought, and the idea made her thoroughly uncomfortable. So much for 'it wasn't me'.

It was at that moment Emma knew beyond doubt that Ruby had intentionally hurt her brother. Somehow, and for some reason, Ruby wasn't Ruby any more and hadn't been since Saunders had left them.

Chapter Seventeen

So you want me to stop Saunders, or whatever he is, to prevent a demon war from destroying the world," Joey said. "Is that right?"

"It's a bit simplistic, but that's more or less right," Remick confirmed.

"Thought so." Joey paused as if he was thinking about it. "Are you out of your mind? I'm seventeen, Remick. What the hell am I supposed to do?"

"That is unclear, I'm afraid," Remick said. "But you're not alone. There is a reason why you are here, why you are all here. Emma too, and you, Raj. Possibly even Anna and the two children. When the end comes, I think you will all play a part. I wouldn't be surprised if our canine friend here even has a role."

As if she knew she was being talked about, Misha woofed once and wagged her tail.

"But a word of warning. You are not the only people who have found themselves in this world. Most are here accidentally and are bewildered to be here, but there are some who may be more important."

"Saunders told us about an old woman he met," Joey recalled. "She was the one who told him I had to come here."

"That was me," Remick said. "I had to give him some hope of finding his escape so he would send you back here. I think he's getting to the point where he will no longer be fooled by a glamour like that, but at the time it served its purpose."

"There's also someone going round shooting," Raj said. "He's killed once and tried to shoot Misha. Joey thought it might have been this Dave. I'm not so sure about that, but I don't think we should get carried away and forget him."

"Saunders may have already found him," Remick warned. "There is someone on their way to him, but Saunders is doing his best to mask him from me. You need to be very careful from here, Joey. Saunders is dangerous and devious and will try anything."

"I don't know about you, Joey," Raj said, "but I don't find that very reassuring."

Remick turned away slightly and thought before he spoke again. "You are all equipped to deal with this. You're here for a reason. The abilities you have acquired make you different from the other people who have found their way here. I first noticed it with Emma—the way her scars warn her of danger. And how did she get those scars? Raj, you can transport yourself and others too by willing it. You wondered if it was connected with your sleepwalking. Young Evan was used to keeping himself from being noticed by his stepfather. Here, he can do it literally. Something which would have been viewed as a flaw in the world you have come from has become an advantage here, and I really don't know why."

"What about me?" Joey asked. "It's my heart, isn't it?"

"It may very well be," Remick replied. "I'm fairly sure it brought you here and brought you here for a reason. I think the reason will become clear. It may also take you home again."

"Can't *you* send us home, Remick?" Joey asked in response. "I'm not up to this. I can't do it. If your people made this place, surely you can get us home? There must be someone better for the job."

"I wish I could, Joey. Believe me, if I had my choice of an army to raise against Saunders, it probably would not consist of six people and a dog. Not when those people include two children and two others who are not much more than children themselves. But sometimes things are as they are, and it is not for me to question."

"You sound more like a civil servant than a demon," Raj observed. "Blaming the rules for not being able to help."

"There is an order to things," Remick said cryptically. "But now I've told you all I can. You need to go. Emma, Anna and the children will need you. It is hard to be completely sure, but I feel that Saunders may already have taken one of the children."

"*Taken?*" Joey was horrified. "Taken how?"

"I believe he has influence over the girl and she is acting for him. I hope Emma and Anna can deal with it, but all the same, I suggest you hurry."

"It would be easier to hurry if you hadn't insisted on walking everywhere," Joey said.

"You don't need to walk any more," Remick said. "You have Raj."

"What? Oh, no," Raj protested. "I can't do that. I've only ever moved short distances, and only then by accident. I don't know how I do it."

"Have you ever tried?"

"No, but I don't think I can learn quickly enough to transport two of us and Misha from here to bloody Pendle Hill!"

Remick took a couple of steps closer to Raj and placed a hand on his forehead. "It's in here," he said. "The knowledge, the ability. It's all in here."

He stepped away. Raj turned to Joey, and Joey briefly saw a strange blue light flicker in Raj's brown eyes, like the reflection of a passing police car.

"Come on, then," Raj said. "Misha, here, girl!"

The dog trotted over and sat obediently next to Raj's leg, her head leaning against his waist.

"Joey, you'll have to take my hand." Joey did so, and Raj laid his hand on Misha's head. "Okay. Let's do this."

And suddenly, they weren't there any more.

***

The man calling himself Remick stared at the place where they had been and then turned away and began to trudge off along the beach.

"I hope you know what you're doing," he said to nobody in particular.

Chapter Eighteen

O N THE ROAD again. Evan showed no sign of ever having been injured; Ruby was behaving just like Ruby; Anna seemed to have found strength from being able to do the job she did in the real world...

And Emma did not trust any of it.

As they walked through the silent streets of the outskirts of Preston, Emma watched them all. There were still too many questions for her liking, and no answers at all. Did Ruby deliberately try to injure her brother? If she did, why did she do it? Had Anna developed miraculous healing powers? That was the only possible explanation for what had happened back at the pub. But, like all the explanations for what happened in this world, it was the one which made least sense. One thing was for sure: it had done wonders for Anna's confidence. Maybe she had healed herself at the same time.

It was Ruby who troubled Emma most. Since they'd left the pub and started on their way again, she seemed to be sticking to Evan like glue. For someone who had not seemed the least bit concerned about his injury, she now appeared to be guarding him jealously. For want of any explanations, Emma resolved to watch and wait in the hope she could react in time if anything happened.

***

Anna felt great—better than she had for as long as she could remember. There was something coursing through her veins better than any drug. It was like the euphoria she had felt some days at work when—despite the long hours, the working conditions and the bad days—she truly believed she was making a difference. Somehow, she had healed Evan's wound, and it made her wonder what else she could do. She felt alive for the first time in a very long time. It was like this was something she was born to do.

As they passed through the edges of the town and back onto the main road through the Lancashire countryside, the landscape became dominated by the long grey shape of Pendle Hill. It was still some way in the distance, but unmistakable and ominous.

"There it is," Emma gestured with a sweep of the arm. "Welcome to witch country."

"I've been here before," Anna said. "Came with some mates on Hallowe'en a couple of years ago. We thought it would be a laugh. You know, see if we could spend the night on Pendle Hill?"

"Did you do it?" Emma asked.

"Sort of. Turned out a load of other people had the same idea, so we started having a bit of a party. Then it began to piss down so we all went home."

"Didn't see any witches, then?"

"Nothing. It felt a bit spooky, but I think that's because we expected it to. It's a funny place. There's shops selling souvenirs, like cuddly witches and stuff for the kids. But if you read the real story of the Pendle witches, it's just kind of sad. A bunch of women got killed for nothing. They were healers, that sort of thing. Two families arguing over territory, and it got out of hand. They weren't witches at all."

"Won't we see any witches?" Evan asked. He'd dropped back to join them, interested in the conversation.

"There are no witches, sweetheart," Anna reassured him. "It's just stories."

"But you fixed my foot," Evan said. "You made it better. Are you magic?"

"I'm not a witch!" Anna laughed.

"You said they were healers."

"Well, maybe I am," Anna said, still laughing. "I'll get myself a broomstick and a black cat!"

"They burn witches."

That was Ruby, who had come over with Evan but until then had been listening silently.

"They used to," Emma agreed. "That's because they didn't understand."

"If you're a witch, they'll burn *you*." Ruby's little face was grim, her eyes glaring and her mouth a hard line.

"I'm not really a witch. I was only joking, Ruby."

"Don't let them see," Ruby said, sounding older than her years. "They'll burn you." She glared at Anna for a second or two longer, then her face changed, and she was Ruby again. She ran off onto the grass verge by the side of the road, calling to Evan to join her.

***

Evan looked up at Emma and Anna, and for the first time, Emma saw something in his eyes which worried her and made her feel sad. He was frightened of his sister.

"She's not like Ruby any more," he said. "Can you fix her like you fixed me?"

Emma and Anna exchanged glances.

"We'll try," Anna said.

Ruby was still calling for Evan and starting to sound cross.

"I'd better go," he said. "Don't let her hurt me."

He ran off to join his sister, glancing back as he went, fear still in his eyes.

"What in God's name are we going to do about that?" Anna asked.

Emma sighed. "I don't know. She's going to need dealing with. I don't know if I can."

"We'll have to," Anna said. "If it comes down to it, we'll have to."

Chapter Nineteen

A T ABOUT THE same time as Emma was contemplating what to do about Ruby, Joey came to, lying on his side in a field, and promptly vomited violently into the grass. He had to roll over to stop himself from planting his face in his own puke. His wrist ached, sending pain shooting up his arm, and his head felt as though it had been stuffed with cotton wool. And then someone had set the cotton wool on fire. And then kicked him in the head.

He lay on his back on the grass and decided there and then that no matter what, he was never, ever travelling like that again. He looked up at the sky and only then began to wonder where he was. The sky was tinted with streaks of pink, and at first, he wasn't sure if it was sunrise or sunset, until he became aware that his clothes and the grass were damp with dew.

Wow, I've been out of it a long time.

He didn't know how long it had taken to shift from Waterloo to here, but he'd clearly been lying in this field all night. So much for saving time.

Hauling himself into a sitting position, he swallowed a mouthful of bile, doing his best to ignore the acrid taste it left in his mouth. He looked around, trying to get his bearings. He was in a field, that was certain. There was nothing around him but grass and, in the distance, an abandoned tractor. The field was bordered by trees and hedges, and from his current position, he couldn't see beyond them.

So, he was in a field, but he had no idea where the field was. For that matter, he also had no idea where Raj was. Or the dog. He turned his head to scan his surroundings and regretted it immediately; the pain nearly made him black out. He lay back down and waited for the pain to pass.

After a few minutes, when it became clear that the pain was not going anywhere soon, he carefully sat up again and woozily put his hands out to push to his feet. That proved to be another bad idea when his wrist buckled and nearly gave way under him. He steadied himself, then started to stumble off across the field, picking the direction completely at random because he had no idea which way to go. Any direction was about as good as any other one. He headed for a hedge so that he could see what was beyond the field: a stile—out of the question with his wrist—and what his parents always taught him was called a kissing gate. Pausing at the gate to get his breath back, he eased himself through it and emerged onto a rough lane.

The lane crossed a field with no hedge and inclined upwards in the shadow of what was, unmistakably, Pendle Hill.

Joey stared at the vast hill in front of him with only one thought in his still-muzzy head. *Do I really have to climb that?*

***

If Joey had gone left instead of right when he started walking, and gone through a gate at the other end of the field, he would have found Raj straight away. Raj had also been out cold all night and was lying underneath the hedge being guarded by Misha, who had emerged unscathed from the trip and had stayed by his side the whole time. She'd decided enough was enough and was licking Raj's face to wake him up.

Raj was bewildered to be woken up by a large, damp tongue in his face. Just like Joey, the first thing he did was throw up the contents of his guts onto the soil under the hedge. He, too, had a blinding headache. It might not have been quite as severe as Joey's, who had the added pain from his wrist to contend with, but it was bad enough. He batted Misha away and tried to sit up, confused why he couldn't until he realised his jacket sleeve was caught on the hawthorn hedge. The thorns had firmly snagged the cloth, and it took two tugs to free his sleeve. Misha bounced impatiently nearby as he did so.

"All right, girl," Raj muttered. "Give me a minute."

He stood up, then had to bend over with his hands on his knees and breathe deeply to deal with the nausea which swept over him. Straightening up more carefully, he wondered where Joey might be.

"What do you think?" he asked Misha, more to say it out loud than in expectation of an answer. "Where's Joey?"

Misha barked and wagged her tail, but Raj didn't find this answer especially conclusive.

"Not much of a tracker, are you?" he said. "Come on, girl, let's go and see if we can find him. Knowing my luck, he'll have landed in a tree or something."

But Joey didn't appear to be caught in a tree. Or a hedge. Or anywhere in the field.

"Come on," he said to Misha. "You're a dog, for God's sake. Pick up his scent or something."

Misha barked then took off across the field with her nose to the grass.

"I don't believe it," Raj muttered. "She did!"

He followed the dog across the field to a gate at the other end. She seemed very keen to go through; he unlatched it, and she took off across another field, nose down and tail up, and again Raj followed. She led him to a stile, which she climbed rather more easily than he did, and on the other side of the stile, they found Joey, who was standing looking up at Pendle Hill.

Misha greeted Joey like a long-lost friend, and Raj found he was equally pleased to see him. "Sleep well?" he asked with a grin.

"I feel terrible," Joey said. "Never do that again. I'd rather crawl."

"Big, isn't it?" Raj looked up at the hill.

"Too big for me. I don't know what you did, but I can barely walk."

"But you don't have to climb it, do you?" Raj pointed out. "Didn't you say the visions had you in a field with the hill in the background?"

"That was Remick's version. Who knows what to believe now?"

"Well, your destiny's around here somewhere, mate. Your girlfriend probably is too. I really don't think we have far to go now."

***

About a quarter of the way up the hill, concealed in some coarse bushes, someone else was observing them—through the sights of a rifle. Webbsy was delighted with his new toy. It was much better than the handguns he'd used before, although he still had one tucked in his belt. The rifle fitted snugly into his shoulder, as if it had been designed that way. He didn't know where Mr. Saunders had got it from, and didn't care. He carefully lined the sights up on his target and squeezed the trigger.

Chapter Twenty

EMMA HEARD THE shot, but by then it was too late. Half an hour before the shot, she, Anna and the kids had reached the foot of Pendle Hill. There were minor roads which led off the main road, and they could see the gradient starting to rise, but they didn't need to go up.

"The hill was in the background of the visions," she said. "But where?"

They stood by the side of the main road, the hill towering above them, with no idea what to do next.

"How do we even know we're on the right side of the hill?" Anna asked. "What if we have to go over to the other side?"

"Then you'd better be up for a hike." Emma's thoughts were interrupted by Evan suddenly tugging at her hand.

"Ruby's gone!"

"What?" Emma spun around. "Where? Where did she go, Evan?"

Evan pointed to a gate, which was halfway open and seemed to lead to some farmland.

"Through there," he said. "I couldn't stop her. She just went."

"Oh, great." Emma sighed. "We'd better find her. God knows what she's up to."

Together, they headed for the gate and went through it into a field which, in another world, might have been home to cows or sheep, but now stretched emptily towards the foot of the hill. And in the distance was Ruby, walking purposefully away from them. Emma wasn't sure if it was an optical illusion, or the sun lighting up Ruby's blonde hair, but the little girl appeared to be glowing.

"I don't like this," Emma said, unconsciously scratching. "We'd better go after her."

"Emma…" Anna stared at her arms. "What's the matter?"

"It's itching like mad. Come on, we need to get her. But be careful."

They hurried off across the field, calling Ruby's name, but she didn't answer. The girl just kept walking. Emma and Anna's longer legs meant they were gaining on her, with Evan doing his best to keep up with them. But before they had even halved the distance between them, Ruby had reached the other side and disappeared through a gap in the hedge. She was now out of sight. Emma broke into a run, and Anna joined her.

A chill descended; the scars on Emma's arms stopped itching and started to ache in a way she had never felt before.

When they reached the gap in the hedge through which Ruby had vanished, Emma paused. Anna and Evan stopped by her side.

"What is it?" Anna asked.

"My arms," Emma said, wincing with pain. "There's something really bad here. Evan, I need you to stay here and stay safe. Will you do that for me?"

"But Ruby…" he protested.

Emma stooped down to Evan and put her hands on his shoulders. "I'll bring Ruby back, but you must stay here. Promise?"

"I promise," he said uncertainly.

Emma drew him into a hug. Over the top of his head, she said to Anna, "You can stay with him if you want."

Anna shook her head. "I'm coming with you."

"Then let's go." Emma released Evan, and she and Anna went through the gap in the hedge.

It really should have come as no surprise that Ruby was waiting in the next field, and standing behind her, with a hand protectively on her shoulder, was Saunders.

"You made it," he said. "I'm afraid my little friend's efforts to slow you down failed. You just can't get the staff these days. She'll have to go."

"Give her back, Saunders," Emma snarled. "Whatever you've done to her, give her back."

"Yes, of course," Saunders said pleasantly. "Whatever you say."

Emma stared at him, confused. Then Saunders laughed, and it was an ugly laugh.

"Don't be ridiculous," he said, all pleasantness gone from his voice. "I have waited a long time for this. Longer than your minds could possibly understand. Your friend Joey is very close by. He will free me. There is just one obstacle left, which is about to be removed."

It was then that somewhere, not far away, a shot rang out.

"There we go," Saunders said.

Emma and Anna were horrified to see his face start to shift and change, like melting wax. His eyes burned with a crimson fire, and the hand which was still clamped onto Ruby's shoulder began to grow filthy, ragged talons.

"I really hope," the creature that was no longer Saunders said in a voice which could never have been human, "I really hope my friend Webbsy has shot the right one."

Chapter Twenty-One

JOEY HEARD THE shot before he felt it. One minute, he and Raj had been contemplating Pendle Hill and wondering whether to go up it, around it, or what, the next minute, Misha had thrown herself at Raj sending both of them tumbling to the ground. Then a resounding *crack* split the air, and Joey felt like he'd been punched in the chest by a heavyweight boxer. The force knocked him backwards, and he sat down hard. He could barely breathe and had to lie down. Something damp was soaking into his sweatshirt. He tried to move to find out what it was, but it was like there was an elephant sitting on his chest.

Somewhere in the distance, he thought he heard someone calling his name, but he couldn't make out who it was. Then he thought he heard his mother's voice above the noise in his ears that sounded like rushing water. *Listen to your heart*, she was saying, *listen to your heart.*

Joey couldn't hear it, not at first. He tried to concentrate and thought he could hear it, faint, like it was in another room. It sounded like a whisper, not a drumbeat. He listened to his heart as it slowed down and then stopped.

***

Raj's first thought was one of relief, that the shot had missed. Misha, with some kind of foresight, had saved his life. Then, out of the corner of his eye, he saw Joey land hard on the rough surface of the field. Frantically, Raj disentangled himself from Misha— not easy when she seemed to think it was some kind of a game.

Raj pulled himself to his feet and rushed over to where his friend lay prone on the ground. Joey's face was already pale, and getting paler; Raj didn't need medical qualifications to know what the dark stain on the front of Joey's sweatshirt was.

One thing his training had told him was he had to act fast. He'd seen plenty of stabbings and gunshot wounds and knew the dangers of trying CPR on anyone who was bleeding out, and whose heart was pumping blood anywhere other than where it was supposed to go. It was difficult enough with access to blood transfusions and the right equipment, but in a field miles from anywhere it was going to be nearly impossible.

But nearly impossible was not impossible, and Raj had no intention of just giving up. He took off his sweatshirt and balled it, pressing it tight to the wound in Joey's chest, and then started compressions. After the first set, he paused and put his face close to Joey's, listening for breaths.

Joey was breathing, but it was faint and ragged. Raj tried again, rhythmically pressing down on Joey's chest for all he was worth. When he listened to the breathing a second time, it was even fainter, hardly there at all. Deep down, he suspected his efforts were all in vain and Joey was gone, but still he continued until someone grabbed his neck from behind and screamed, "*Get OFF him!*"

***

Emma ran when she heard the shot. She forgot momentarily the horror of the thing that Saunders had become. She forgot that this thing was still holding onto Ruby. She forgot everything apart from one thought—*Joey*—and ran. Once or twice, she almost stumbled on the uneven ground, but it didn't slow her down. She ran through an open gate from one field to the next. There, she saw Joey, lying on his back, and another man leaning over him, beating him up.

She didn't even pause; she just seized the other man around the neck and yelled, "*Get OFF him!*" as loudly as she could down his ear.

The other man struggled with Emma, but at the same time carried on with what he was doing. "I'm trying to save him, you idiot," he snapped. "I'm a doctor."

Emma let go and stepped back. "Seriously?"

"Seriously," the man gasped between pushes on Joey's chest. "I'm…Raj…I'm guessing…you're Emma."

Emma stared, but this other man—Raj—stopped pummelling Joey and sat back on his heels.

"And I'm afraid you're too late," he said.

"What do you mean?" Emma demanded. "No! Carry on! Don't stop!"

She felt a hand on her shoulder and turned to see Anna had followed her.

"He's gone, Emma," Raj said. "I'm so sorry."

"*No!*" Emma shouted. "Anna, do something!"

Anna put her arms round Emma. "I don't know if I can."

"*Do something!*" Emma insisted. "You fixed Evan, so fix Joey!"

"I don't even know how I did it. And if he's dead—"

"He's not dead!" Emma cried. "Don't say that! He's not dead. You've got to try."

Anna gently pulled herself away from Emma and moved over to Joey.

Raj moved away so she could kneel next to Joey's body. "I don't know what you've got that I haven't," he said, "but be my guest."

Anna laid her hands on Joey's chest and prayed.

The air filled with the stench of burning flesh, and the shooting began again.

Chapter Twenty-Two

F ROM HIS HIDING place in plain sight by the hedge, Evan heard the first shot, and saw Emma and Anna run. For a while, the ugly burning man-thing stayed where it was, still with its hand on Ruby's shoulder. Then there were more bangs, and it turned its head, sniffed the air like a dog, and followed, half floating, half flying in the direction Emma and Anna had gone. As soon as the thing took its hand off Ruby's shoulder, she dropped to the ground.

As the burning thing took off across the field, Evan left his hiding place and hurried over to his sister. Ruby lay on her side on the grass, but when Evan shook her shoulder, she stirred and opened her eyes to look at him. Her eyes were clear and blue, and Evan knew that Ruby was Ruby again. He helped her to her feet.

She looked confused for a moment, and then frowned, tears starting in her eyes. "Evan, I hurt you." Her lips trembled but Evan hugged her tight.

"It's okay. It wasn't you. It was him. It's okay."

"I can still hear him in my head. I know what he wants. He wants to kill them."

"We won't let him," Evan said. "He can't see me. Come on. We've got to stop him now."

***

When the shooting started again, Raj hit the ground. A bullet thudded into the soil beside him, shattering a clod of earth and showering him with dirt. Then another bullet ricocheted off a rock nearby. Raj hardly dared lift his head, but when he heard the sound of barking receding into the distance as Misha took off up the hill, he knew he had to do something. He looked around; his backpack was near him but just out of reach, and protruding from the top of the bag was the end of the crowbar he had taken from the garage. He shuffled on his stomach over to his bag, took hold of the crowbar and…

…jumped…

…and found himself standing behind what looked like a teenager in a hoodie, who was pointing a rifle towards Misha, who was speeding up the hill.

"You're not shooting her again, you bastard," Raj said and brought the crowbar down on the teenager's head. The shot went wide. Before the kid in the hoodie could move, Raj hit him again, hard. This time, he stayed down.

Raj stared at the kid, barely able to comprehend what his rage had made him do. *I just killed someone.* Then the kid moaned and stirred. *Alive, but no threat.*

At that moment, Misha burst through a bush and greeted Raj by putting her paws on his chest, nearly knocking him off his feet. He stroked her huge head and then pushed her down. At the bottom of the hill, he could see Anna still kneeling over Joey, and Emma standing to one side. But he could also see something out of a nightmare floating across the field towards them, singeing the grass as it went.

***

Anna laid her hands on Joey's chest and tried to feel something, *anything*. All she could feel was that her hands were wet and she knew without looking they were wet with blood. She closed her eyes and concentrated, attempting to remember how it had felt when she healed Evan's foot. The trouble was, she really didn't remember feeling anything much other than that tingle. It just happened, and it was only a cut foot. This was…well, this was almost certainly a corpse.

"I don't know what I'm doing," she said, turning to Emma. As she did, she picked up a smell like a barbecue gone terribly wrong, and acrid smoke stung her nostrils. Behind Emma, a vision from Hell had appeared. The figure of what could have been a man was floating a foot or so above the ground.

"You had better figure out what you're doing quickly," it said in a voice like a collapsing bonfire. "If he dies, so do you."

Chapter Twenty-Three

ANNA THOUGHT AT first it was the heat from the burning man which was making her feel warm, or at the very least, her sense of panic at his words. But then she understood that the warmth was radiating from her hands and from Joey's chest underneath them. She could have sworn she saw a flicker of light coming from inside the hole in his chest. Glancing up at Emma, she caught her eye, nodding almost imperceptibly, and kept her hands on Joey's sternum, whispering, "Come on, come on," under her breath.

Then Joey startled everyone by coughing once, then again, and then sitting upright. He looked around, squinting at Anna's face as if trying to recall where he had seen it before, coughed again and started to struggle to his feet.

Anna tried to hold him down. "Stay still. You were shot."

"I'm fine," Joey replied, his voice hoarse. "I think."

As soon as he spoke, Emma rushed over to him and threw her arms around him, almost pushing Anna out of the way as she did so. "You're alive," she cried.

"Just about. Don't know how." He took hold of her arms and gently moved her away from him. "You need to stand back. I think there's something coming out of me."

Joey took several paces away from her. His heart was pounding, and it felt like his whole body was vibrating with the rhythmic *thud thud*. As his heart beat its relentless rhythm in his head, he became aware of his connection to this world and other worlds, just out of reach, as if he were glimpsing them out of the corner of his eye.

A beam of white light flooded out of his chest, and he jerked back. He could feel it pouring from him, unstoppable, powerful and magnificent. The beam hit the air a few feet away, like it had encountered an invisible wall, and fanned out, forming a rough square maybe eight foot high. It stopped spreading, and a crack appeared in the centre of it.

"What the hell is *that*?" Anna asked in astonishment.

"That," the Saunders thing said, floating forwards, "is my freedom. It was *him*. He was the key."

***

From halfway up the hill, Raj watched, unable to believe what he was seeing. Joey was alive, standing up and apparently projecting a beam of pure white light into the air in front of him. If he was surprised by that, he was even more astonished when he looked down and saw a small, blonde-haired boy standing next to him, smiling and holding a finger to his lips.

***

The Saunders-thing floated closer to Joey, its flames burning brighter.

"Open it!" it hissed. "Open the portal and let me be free!"

But Joey couldn't move. The beam coming out of his chest had him rooted to the spot. Something nudged his hand and he just about registered the fact that Evan was next to him, offering him a crowbar. He tried to grasp it, but his wrist was still weak, and he dropped it. Then Evan and the crowbar were gone, and the hideous Saunders-creature's shrieking came back into focus.

"OPEN IT! Open it now or I will burn them all!"

Emma stepped between the burning thing and Joey. "Leave him alone! You've hurt him enough!"

"I don't intend to hurt him, girl," the creature said. "Not until I'm free. But when I go through the portal, this world will serve no purpose and cease to be. And so will you."

As if in answer, the sky began to darken, and the ground started to vibrate.

"You're not going through there," Emma threatened. "We'll fight you. Come on! Bring on your Screamers. Joey's beaten them before!"

"I have no need of them." The Saunders-thing gave a hideous laugh. "I could burn you all with a thought."

"Then why haven't you?" Emma shouted. "Come on! What are you waiting for?"

Something nudged her, and she was about to slap it away when she realised Evan had reappeared, unnoticed, by her side. He placed the end of a solid, iron crowbar in her hand. She winked at him and rushed forwards, plunging the sharp end of the crowbar into the fiery centre of the Saunders-thing's chest. It screamed and staggered backwards, but Emma hung on, pushing the crowbar with all her might. She just had time to register that it was lunging towards the crack which the beam of light from Joey's chest had opened.

With one flaming hand, the creature lashed out, catching Emma full force in the side of the head, then disappeared, shrieking, through the hole in the sky. Hair and clothes scorched and smouldering, Emma was thrown violently backwards onto the grass, where she lay still.

Chapter Twenty-Four

THEN EMMA WINRUSH died.

Chapter Twenty-Five

JOEY TRIED TO get to Emma, but the shaking ground sent him stumbling to his knees. The beam which had projected the portal onto the air was cut off as he fell, yet the portal remained.

Raj saw Emma collapse and started to race down the hill, Misha running alongside. The whole hill was shuddering, and he had to dodge tumbling rocks as he ran.

Anna was first to Emma's side, but a quick glance told her she was too late. Blood freely trickled from Emma's nose and ear, and a section of her hair was burnt away completely. Anna fell to her knees and hugged the body of her friend to her, trying to feel something—*anything*—to take hold of and heal.

"I can't do it," she sobbed. "I can't! There's nothing there."

Evan and Ruby could do nothing but cling to each other as the turf beneath their feet began to shake.

For a while, no-one had anything to say. Then Joey, who had managed to get to his feet, spoke.

"You need to get out of here. Raj, Anna, take the kids and Misha and go."

He picked up his discarded backpack and opened it. He pulled out a stuffed badger which he handed to Ruby. "Thank you, Ruby. He's looked after me well."

"What about you?" Anna asked, tears flowing freely down her cheeks.

Joey limped over and took Emma's body from her.

"I'll be following. I'm going to bring Emma home."

Raj shook Joey's hand. "Take care, mate. We'll see you on the other side."

Raj took Ruby by the hand, and Anna held Evan's hand tightly and, with Misha at their heels, they stepped through the portal and were gone.

Joey put one arm under Emma's back, and the other underneath her legs. Ignoring the pain screaming at him from his wrist, he lifted her, surprised to find out how little she weighed. Then he kissed her once on her cold lips, said "Come on. Let's go home," and, as the world behind him began to tear itself apart, he walked through the portal.

The portal immediately began to contract until, little by little, it too disappeared.

Epilogue

JOEY WOKE UP with sand in his mouth and a dull ache in his chest. At first, he had no idea where he was, but, as he lifted himself up, he could see the unmistakable iron statues of Crosby beach standing like sentinels in the early morning mist. In the distance, he'd swear he saw, if only for a brief moment, the figure of a long-haired man in a leather jacket walking away into the mist. The figure even appeared to wave.

The thought hit Joey like a sledgehammer to his chest. *Emma!* He looked around, but there was no sign of her, and his heart ached for that too.

There was no sign of his bag. He was wearing the sweatshirt and jeans he had been wearing on Pendle Hill, what seemed like a lifetime ago. He began to wonder whether he had dreamed everything, but the residual pain in his wrist as he pushed up from the sand told him differently. Then he heard birdsong, beautiful, miraculous birdsong, and he knew he was finally home.

There were people taking dogs for an early morning walk. Real, ordinary people! Joey smiled at each one as he passed them by. All he wanted to do was get back to his house and his parents. He walked and walked until his feet hit pavement and he was minutes away from home. There were cars moving, their headlights piercing the mist—he had never been so glad to see traffic in his life. Then he was there. His street. He could see his house. He opened the gate and automatically fumbled in his pocket for his keys, which, by some miracle were still there. His heart pounding with excitement, he inserted his key in the lock.

But his key wouldn't turn. He tried again, and again; still he could not unlock the door. Thinking maybe his key had been damaged somehow, he took it out of the lock and knocked on the door. He stood back and waited until a light came on in the house.

The door opened, and a sleepy-looking man stood there.

It was not Joey's father. The man was at least ten years older and had a beard where Ian Cale was clean-shaven.

"Who are you?" the man asked sharply. "What do you want?"

"I…I…I'm sorry," Joey stammered and backed away.

As he hurried down the road, Joey tried to work out what had happened. Had he moved in time? Was this another time in which his parents had sold the house? Then he thought about different presidents and actors and brands of coffee, and with a sense of vertigo realised that maybe he had not come back to the home he knew at all.

It was then that he nearly collided with someone hurrying around the corner. He mumbled an apology and saw a flash of purple hair.

"Emma?"

To Be Continued

About the Author

Liverpool born Bob Stone is an author and bookshop owner. He has been writing for as long as he could hold a pen and some would say his handwriting has never improved. He is the author of two self-published children's books, *A Bushy Tale* and *A Bushy Tale: The Brush Off*. *Missing Beat*, the first in a trilogy for Young Adults, is his first full-length novel.

Bob still lives in Liverpool with his wife and cat and sees no reason to change any of that.

By the Author

A Bushy Tale

A Bushy Tale: The Brush Off

Missing Beat